Frank Trollope

Old Times Revived

A novel. Part 2

Frank Trollope

Old Times Revived
A novel. Part 2

ISBN/EAN: 9783337045951

Printed in Europe, USA, Canada, Australia, Japan

Cover: Foto ©Andreas Hilbeck / pixelio.de

More available books at **www.hansebooks.com**

FORTUNE'S WHEEL

A NOVEL

BY

ALEX. INNES SHAND

AUTHOR OF
'AGAINST TIME,' 'LETTERS FROM WEST IRELAND,' ETC.

IN THREE VOLUMES
VOL. III.

WILLIAM BLACKWOOD AND SONS
EDINBURGH AND LONDON
MDCCCLXXXVI

CONTENTS OF THE THIRD VOLUME.

FORTUNE'S WHEEL.

CHAPTER XXX.

THE POET IN THE PROVINCES.

"Come to the 'Falcon,' Ralph, and sit down a little," said Jack Venables, with unwonted tenderness. "It does not matter much by what train we go back to town, since you can only go north by the night express."

But already beginning to recover from the shock which had stunned him, Ralph merely shook his head. And when Jack repeated the suggestion as they stepped ashore, he said, "No; movement is the best thing for me now. As yet, I dare not sit still and think."

Indeed the blow that had struck him so unseasonably was a heavy one, and might well shake his manhood for the moment. Yet though the contents of the telegram were most unexpected, there was nothing sensationally unnatural in them. The illness he had made light of had taken a serious turn. Mrs Leslie had an attack of inflammation of the lungs; and although, knowing all the circumstances, she had expressed no wish to see her son, yet the relative in attendance on her had felt bound to telegraph.

"Thank heaven, the telegram reached me in time," moaned Ralph, as he kept firm hold of Jack's arm. "Though I would to God Grace had not fainted. *He* knows I have enough to bear without that."

"As to Grace fainting," said Jack, "you could hardly have expected or wished anything else. Think how sudden it all was. The dear girl is not of iron, as you know; and you yourself, with all your nerve, have been very sufficiently shaken. Grief of that kind does not hurt, and the worst that can possibly happen is that the pleasure of her voyage will be spoiled. She will remember, on second thoughts, that she leaves you in perfect health; and will look forward to your being soon reunited—possibly by the next steamer."

"It is not of Grace I am thinking," said poor Ralph, rather inconsistently, "it is my mother."

Though indeed his predominant feeling was one of bitter self-reproach at having made light of the illness which he now exaggerated. Heartless and ungrateful son as he had been, he was very deservedly punished. There too, Jack, understanding his feelings, was ready to act the comforter, and he spoke with a decision of purpose that was not without its effect.

"My dear fellow, you see everything in sinister lights at present, and no wonder. But for your own sake, and for Grace's, and above all for Mrs Leslie's, do not give way to morbid self-reproach. You know as well as I, that no mortal could have foreseen this. Influenzas are of everyday occurrence, and you have always told me that your mother's constitution is excellent. You have nothing to reproach yourself with, and even now there is

every reason to hope that her strength will
throw off the illness. I know something of
both your pluck and your Christianity. Take
comfort and courage, and put your trust in
Providence. In a few days you may look
back upon all this as only a cause for gratitude. In a few days Mrs Leslie may be
pronounced out of danger. In a few days
you will certainly have a reassuring telegram
from Gibraltar, whither you can send any
messages you please. Meantime, I need not
tell you to be a man ; but remember you have
a journey before you, and a trying meeting at
the end of it. You will dine with me quietly
in my rooms, and I shall either see you safe
off from King's Cross or go with you to Scotland, as you prefer."

Mr Venables felt rather abroad in the unfamiliar character of the preacher, but he was
pleased to see the good effect of his words.
Leslie did turn his thoughts to Providence,
and resolved in calm acquiescence to brace
himself for the better or the worse. With
great external composure, though in profoundly
melancholy mood, he entered the railway car-
riage with the rest of the party. Nor was that

effort, though perhaps unnecessary, without its immediate reward. Sir Stamford, to whom Miss Winstanley had been paying court in the meantime, had been really touched by the tragic little incident to which she had given him the clue. With his many weaknesses, he was a good-natured man. He had taken an opportunity of whispering with his brother director; and on taking leave of Leslie in London, he stammered out some words he meant for sympathy, though he was embarrassed by having been bound over to secrecy. Then he added, that if Mr Leslie pleased to arrange matters with Mr Moray, the Board would gladly give him any reasonable leave of absence before taking up his appointment. So far as he could judge, on brief acquaintance, both the Board and the Resident would gladly submit to some temporary inconvenience, to secure the assistance of so capable a gentleman.

Ralph made Sir Stamford a friend for life, by thanking him with real fervour. Indeed before the chairman knew that he was helping forward a true love affair, it had struck him that a man of Leslie's stamp might have done

much better, and that he was stooping to take
this secretaryship in the far south.   As for
Leslie, the chairman's timely thoughtfulness
came as a great relief.   It would have added
infinitely to the pains of suspense, had he
feared that his appointment might be filled
up in the meantime — had the sentence of
separation been indefinitely protracted• by
depriving him of the reason for going to
Sumatra as an inmate of the Resident's
house.

He did not choose to let Jack accompany
him to the north, but nevertheless he had a
travelling companion.   When poor Donald
knew that it was Miss Grace who had fainted,
he was thrown into terrible trouble.   Swoons
are serious things in the Highlands, where
they mean the shattering of an oak rather
than the bending of a sapling, and it took a
good deal to reassure him.   Then he transferred his anxiety to the young laird of Roodholm with whom he had a fellow-feeling in the
circumstances.

It might be that Mr Venables was right.
He dared to say he knew a deal about many
things.   But if Miss Grace were but to twist

her little finger, she was worth making a work about; and he liked Mr Leslie all the better for it, and him with his mind, too, "full of his mother."

Donald looked so wistfully forlorn when they reached London, that Jack willingly assented to a suggestion of Leslie's, and asked him to join them at dinner in his rooms. When this humble friend understood that he was actually invited to sit down at table with "the gentlemen," although immensely flattered, he protested strongly and resisted stoutly. But Jack would not be denied; and he had a winningly commanding way with him in the circumstances.

"Hoot, Donald, man; it won't be the first time by many that you and Mr Leslie and I have eaten and drunk together. It's no use your saying that it was different on the hillside: so far as I can see, there isn't a hair of difference. Besides," he added confidentially, " you will be doing him a real kindness. He and I have had our cracks out; and we mustn't let him go on talking about melancholy subjects. You come and dine, and bring Bran, and we will carry him away among

us to Lochrosque and Glenconan, and freshen
him up a bit for his travel."

"Then in troth, Mr Venables, I will do as
you wish.   But there was one other thing, sir,
that I had been thinking of."

" What was that, Donald ? "

" It was just this, sir.   I was thinking that
Mr Leslie would be lonesome-like through the
night; and he's not looking altogether himself, moreover.   And they'll be wanting me
down at Glenconan ; and I have done all that
I came south to do, and seen as much as I had
wished.   So I was thinking that I would be
taking the same train myself, if your honours
had got nothing to say against it."

" But, Donald, my good fellow, you have
never been in London before ; and you must
have a look round the sights before you go
back again."

" 'Deed, sir, and very truly, I have but
small stomach for the sights ; and it is a sore
heart that this day has given me.   No ; I will
be going back to the north this night, though
I would not wish to be any trouble to Mr
Leslie."

" Well, since you will have it, and between

you and me, I really think it a capital idea. And when you come south on your next visit, as you shall do by-and-by, to me, and at my expense—mind that—we shall go and see everything that is worth the seeing. Who knows but you may meet Glenconan and Miss Grace? I should not be surprised for one. Somehow, I don't think they will be long away this time."

"And may God bless you for that word, sir," said Donald, grinning with delight. "And when that day does come, there's but one sight in London I should greatly care for."

To any one who knew nothing of the Highlanders, it would have been strange to see the keeper at the little dinner. A Southern of similar station would have sat awkwardly on the edge of his chair, eaten little, said less, and pained his companions by his awkward embarrassment. Donald Ross, in all essential respects, was the high-bred though simple-mannered Highland gentleman. It almost seemed as if he were trying to set his superiors at their ease, and very entirely he succeeded. Without putting himself forward in the least, he spoke

manfully and modestly. Jack and he at first
sustained the conversation; but Leslie, who
had sat listening, gradually joined in. When
he spoke of things in the north, of course
Donald was at home; and when Jack drew
him out on his impressions of travel and the
metropolis, his quaint but intelligent remarks
were irresistibly amusing. Nothing Venables
could have devised could have done Leslie
more good, or so quickly restored the manly
tone of his mind. So much so, that when he
was told of Donald's proposal, he was by no
means too proud to acknowledge that he
should be glad to have his stanch hill-friend
as a travelling companion. "He and Bran
are like things belonging to Grace," he said
afterwards to Jack, half apologetically. But
he made it a condition that Donald should
spend the rest of his leave as a guest under
his mother's roof at Roodholm.

"You won't have a merry time of it,
Donald, worse luck; but I could never let
you go by my door-step. We do not meet
with friends like you every day, and when
we do come across them, we are bound to
make much of them."

And if Donald could have made himself easy about Miss Grace, it was himself, as he might have said, would have been the happy man that night.

As for things at Roodholm, they were better than Leslie could have hoped. Thanks to her constitution and to excellent nursing, Mrs Leslie had been pronounced out of immediate danger. Leeches had pulled her through, but she was greatly weakened by the attack; for she had suffered much, and still suffered intensely, from the thought of the ruin she had innocently brought on her brother and his daughter.

"Were her mind once at ease, Mr Ralph," said the old country doctor, "she would want little of our medicine or yet of our looking after. As it is, and at her time of life, we will have an uphill job before we see her herself again; but you will be a better doctor than me, and it was just her salvation that telegram catching you before you started."

Mr Ralph was much of the same opinion. His mother professed herself grieved at his having come back; at his having jeoparded his

appointment, and separated from his cousin—
for it need hardly be said that her maternal
sagacity had long before penetrated the secret
of his attachment.   But each look and action
contradicted the words, and her evident joy
in his society, with the caresses that evinced
it, more than repaid him for the sorrows of
the separation.   Moreover, as Jack had fore-
told, the telegram came from Gibraltar.   Telegrams must be matter-of-fact things at best.
Even if you cast considerations of economy to
the winds, and launch out like the special
correspondent of a crack journal, it is impossible to flash our finer feelings along the
wires, submitting them to the scrutiny of
telegraph officials and local postmasters.   Yet
Grace, with a woman's wit, and a loving
girl's affectionate sympathy, had contrived so
to word her despatch that her lover might
read between the lines.   They had been sadly
disappointed, she said, but she was wonder-
fully well; and altogether he had every reason to be satisfied.   There was no hope expressed of his joining them speedily; but
that, as he felt, must have been out of the
question.   It was impossible that Grace, either

directly or indirectly, should say anything to induce him to leave his mother's sick-bed. Next, in due course, came letters from Port Said, both from Moray and his daughter. The cordiality of the former, the more than cousinly warmth of the latter, left nothing indeed to desire. Moray spoke of his nephew, and his regard for him, in terms more flattering than he had ever used before. He could write in the circumstances as he never could have spoken. Not having his nephew's assistance on landing in Sumatra, he felt to be a grievous personal loss ; but should Leslie see his way to carrying out their plans, his presence would be doubly welcome. As for Grace, though naturally she hinted nothing directly of the engagement which did not exist, she wrote almost in the character of a betrothed bride longing to comfort a bereaved lover. And her gentle sympathy was almost more grateful than the assurances she insinuated of eternal fidelity. As Ralph read the note again and again, he was raised into a seventh heaven of delight : and he remembered the words of the sage Mr Venables, who had predicted precisely what had occurred. To be sure, on second thoughts he accused himself of heartlessness : did not his mother continue in a critical state? But after all, Mrs Leslie was steadily, if slowly, getting on : so long as he was with her, progress seemed probable ; and he was determined of course that, cost what it might, he should stay by her till he had seen her health re-established.

So he set himself down and wrote a letter to Sir Stamford Scraper, with something of the guile of the serpent, as well as the gentleness of the dove. He explained that for the present he was not his own master, although his mother had been pronounced out of danger, and was doing better than he could have hoped. He spoke of the enthusiasm with which he had entered the Company's service, and added that it would be with deep regret he should resign himself to renounce his prospects. He quoted a passage or two from his uncle's letter, to indicate the Resident's feelings in the matter. He thanked Sir Stamford gratefully for his kind expressions when they had met and parted the other day ; but added that he could not think of holding him to offers made under the pressure of kindly excitement.

The answer came in course of post, worded very much as our friend had expected. Each sentence was characteristic of the writer, as Leslie or any one else might have read him :—

"SUMATRA COLONISATION COMPANY,
303 LEADENHALL STREET.

"DEAR SIR,—I duly received yours of the 17th current. You will permit me to remark, that had we been better acquainted, you would probably have felt it unnecessary to make a proposition, which—as I am bound to say, and I trust you will forgive me for saying it— reflects in no inconsiderable degree on my character as a man of business and a gentle- man. I never use words in matters of business without weighing them carefully; and as it has been my boast that my word is as good as my bond, I have never been known to go back from a promise. Having premised so much, in the way of essential self- vindication, I may add that otherwise your feelings do you the greatest credit, and con- firm the high opinion I had formed of you,

being, as I flatter myself, no indifferent judge
of human nature. I said that we were desir-
ous of securing your services, and I am glad
to take this opportunity of repeating the statement. If you communicate with our secretary,
and inform him of the address of your bankers,
your pay will be placed duly to your credit in
the meantime. The appointments begin from
the day of your disembarking in the colony.
I learn with extreme gratification that your
anxieties have been relieved with regard to
your mother's illness,—and I have the honour,
dear sir, to remain," &c., &c.

Pompous like himself as was the chairman's
communication, the recipient was greatly
pleased with it. His plans must depend on
Mrs Leslie's health, but otherwise he was left
master of his movements. Nor was the passage as to the pay the least agreeable part.
The pay was not great, nor was Leslie a
covetous man. But, as we know, he was
sinking the bulk of his modest rental in a
reserve fund against probable calls by the
liquidators of the bank; and his ailing mother,
who felt as strongly as himself on the subject,

had been stinting her expenditure and re-
trenching on her jointure. He felt he could
use this new source of income with a clear
conscience—it might have puzzled him to say
how he drew the distinction, but so it was—
as he had not hesitated to spend his occasional
literary gains. And now the thought of his
unfinished poem occurred to him. He had
leisure on his hands; he needed interest and
occupation. He threw himself into the interrupted work with renewed energy, rising to it
like a giant refreshed after his long literary
repose. He was delighted to find that inspiration had not failed him; if it was less fever-
ishly ardent, perhaps it was all the more
healthy. Fresh from a long walk or ride, he
would correct and revise the manuscript that
had been flung aside from his feverish fingers
in these vigils in Jermyn Street; and as he
took up the threads he had dropped, and as
he retwisted them, to his infinite satisfaction
he admired his own work. In a rush of mingled and melancholy associations, he seemed
to recognise the vivid truthfulness of scenes
and situations, and, above all, of the por-
traiture of himself and of her who had been

at once the pole-star of his affections and his
muse. He toned down the egotism, he touched
up the traits of the muse, he chastened some
of the more audaciously high-flown metaphors,
and generally acted the unsparing critic. But
the music of his verses went ringing through
his soul, and the chords began to vibrate as
before, though more calmly and none the less
sweetly. He changed the manner of his
treatment, though not the themes; and again,
with the fancies fast gathering between times
in his brain, his fingers flew over the paper.
Working early, before his mother was visible
—and late, after she and the household had
retired to rest—he covered the ground at a
pace which almost startled himself, and the
work was rapidly drawing to a conclusion.
Considering that the success of his smaller
pieces had paved the way, he began to dream
of fame and of growing popularity, and of
driving more profitable bargains with the
booksellers. Indeed one of these gentlemen,
and not the least eminent in "the Row,"
chancing to hear confidentially and "acci-
dentally," through Jack Venables, that the
clever author of 'The Idyls of the North' had

a new work on the stocks, had already sent
him a diplomatic note on the subject, marked
" private and confidential."   And he hoped
fondly that, in the course of a very few
weeks, he might make his final arrangements
in the matter, on his way through London to
Sumatra.   Should his 'Rosabelle' have the
success he hoped, it would be doubly sweet
to hear of it where his cousin, his bride, could
wreathe the laurels for his brow; while, on
the other hand, should it turn out that he
had deceived himself, Grace might be trusted
to console him for the disappointment.   For
now — without a single spoken word — he
absolutely confided in her affection.

CHAPTER XXXI.

A LION IN LONDON.

LESLIE went to London a month or two later, although not with the intention of starting immediately for Sumatra. His mother was still so delicate, that he did not dare to exile himself to the antipodes. With her son within reach, she was likely to mend and do well; but the shock of an indefinite separation might slowly though surely prove fatal. Not for the sake of Grace herself could he have left England under the circumstances. Meanwhile, and tolerably hopeful and contented, he had enough to occupy his mind. A second heavy call had been made by the bank liquidators, and under the fullest powers of attorney from his uncle, he had been realising assets to meet the payments. That was disagreeable, though not unexpected; and assuredly the business was eminently prosaic. But on the other hand, his poem was to appear, and his publishers were even more sanguine of success than the author. It had been submitted, *en petit comité*, to connoisseurs of name and critics of culture. The general verdict had been extraordinarily favourable, and even the objections were rather complimentary than disparaging. It was said that it shared the foolhardiness as well as the inspiration of genius : in the pride and intoxication of unusual power, the poet had ventured on liberties with the public, which the public might either resent or approve. All the same, anticipations in literary circles were excited, and expectations began to stand on tiptoe. The publishers had offered liberal terms, though contingent, in some degree, on the success of the sale. Big men as they were, it was important to them that the book should succeed, and they had done their best to take their measures accordingly. It was to be brought out on the eve of the session, when the town was beginning to fill. And big men as they were, they did not altogether disdain the arts which the illustrious Mr Puff had

reduced to a science in 'The Critic.' Editors
and their literary contributors, half-confidenti-
ally admitted to pleasant little symposia, at
which some pages from the poem gave a
flavour to the claret, proud of being introduced
to that *cercle intime*, printed paragraphs that
were provocative when not positively flattering. In fact, it seemed certain that the
production of 'Rosabelle' would be a literary
event, and it was only natural that the usually
steady-going author should be as excited on
the subject as many other people.

Then, setting empty vaingloriousness aside,
a triumph seemed of no little consequence
to him. Like Sir Walter Scott and other
literary men of smaller stature, he had always
set a low value on literary fame as compared
to more practical successes. He had had the
blessed good fortune to win his cousin's love—
at least he hoped so ; but if she cast in her lot
with his, she sacrificed the brilliant worldly
fortune which Jack Venables could certainly
have offered her. He could never hope to
make money like Mr Jack ; but at all events,
he might offer her something in compensation.
Fame and even flattery would be grateful to

him, could he lay them as tributes at her feet.
Moreover, high poetical fame in those days
transformed itself into solid pudding.   It was
not as in the times when the Troubadours
were merely a better sort of mendicants; when
the Border minstrels and the Highland harpers
were satisfied with a shake-down and "the
run of the table."   If he could cash a handsome cheque from his publishers before steam-
ing to the south, and carry the assurance of
some permanent income from his copyright,
his arrival would be all the more welcome to
Moray, and possibly none the less welcome to
Grace; though he acquitted the goddess of his
dreams of any possible mercenary motives.

So the imaginative and poetical side of his
temperament was in the ascendant as the day
approached when the poem was to appear.
Lockhart tells us that Sir Walter, in similar
circumstances, showed "a manly indifference
to the fate of his literary bantlings," as when
he went cruising with the Commissioners of
Northern Lights among the Hebrides, when
'Waverley' was about to issue from the Bal-
lantyne Press.   Leslie neither felt nor showed
so much manly indifference; but he comprom-

ised. He took the Lake district on his way
from the Lothians to London ; and though it
was in the very depth of an inclement winter,
he went for some days beyond reach of letters,
and refused to look at the metropolitan papers.
It was an odd feeling that possessed him when,
subsequently travelling south, he declined to
deal with the newsboys at Lancaster or Rugby.
He felt himself a fool ; he called himself a coward : all the same he would defer the eventful moment. Yet his resolution was shaken,
and his mind in great measure set at ease,
when he saw a poster of the ' Saturday Review ' on Messrs Smith's bookstall at Rugby.
The place of honour in the literary criticisms
was given to ' Rosabelle, a Poem,' and the
fact told much in his favour in every way.
The Saturday Reviewers would surely never
have rushed into the field, simply to anticipate
the hangman's office, with a book that only
deserved burning. And if by any chance
they had gone out of the way to pillory him,
they had given him an eminently complimentary advertisement in any case.

Unwontedly excited, rather thirsty than
hungry, though the mercury stood at 28°

Fahr., the ordinarily calm Leslie drove to
Jack Venables's rooms. Jack had earnestly
pressed a bed upon him; and Ralph, true to
his system of self-sacrificing economy, had ac-
cepted the offer, though rather against his will.
He loved independence before all things; but
then Jack was always a great deal out of doors.
And he was glad he had given his consent,
when he saw his host's unmistakable pleasure.
The snug dining-room, with its table spread for
a *tête-à-tête* meal, was set out as for a little *fête*.

"My dear fellow," exclaimed Leslie, "you
don't mean that you have kept yourself at
home for my sake? you don't mean that you
have put off your dinner till 9.30?"

"Hang it all, my dear Homer, let us have
no mock modesty. It is not once in the lifetime of many men that it is given to a humble
individual to welcome so distinguished a guest,
my dear Dante, my dear Petrarch. I am not
over-strong in poetry—I only re-echo what I
hear on all sides, so you must forgive my con-
founding my complimentary epithets. You
come with your blushing honours thick upon
you; and upon my own honour, I believe
that they are still impalpable to the wearer.

Can I conceive by any imaginary chance that you have looked at no papers on your way up from Cumberland?"

"That is exactly what I have not done; and now, for heaven's sake, drop hyperbole and be serious. To tell the truth, I am anxious about the book, and I am sure you don't want to trifle with me."

"Not for worlds, old fellow," said Jack, becoming serious at once. "Though I could hardly conceive," he added, with a smile, "your changing parts with me, and doing precisely what I might have done in such circumstances. Well, in a single word, you may have gone into the Lake country obscure, but you have come out to find yourself famous. Wordsworth had not a chance with you. Oh," he went on, in answer to a deprecatory gesture of Ralph's, "don't think I am chaffing. I don't pretend to arrange precedence between you and the poets' William—possibly he may survive as a classic when you have been shelved—all I say is, that he had to pull for a generation or so against the tide of public favour; while you, like Byron, have awakened to find yourself a celebrity. And how proud Grace will be! while even her father will feel he has drawn a prize in his son-in-law. But here comes the dinner in good time, and I for one am hungry enough."

Which was more than Leslie was. The good news, in the absence of all details, had pretty nearly deprived him of appetite. He drank of the carefully warmed claret more freely than was his wont: had it been cognac he might have been gulping it down without tasting it. They had changed the subject during dinner, but his thoughts were far away; and Jack, while the servant was in the room, only talked for talking's sake. When the man left them to the decanters and the devilled biscuits, Jack stepped to the side-table and threw a dozen journals before Leslie. From the 'Times' down to the—from motives of prudence we will not say what—all had treated the poem with marvellous promptitude. One or two had hurriedly reviewed it the very day after publication. It might be due in great measure to the astute diplomacy of Messrs Tonson; all the same, it was a most sensational success for an almost maiden author. Leslie was quite quick-witted enough to see that those who

were envious of long-established reputations
had malevolently taken advantage of an opportunity to exalt a new aspirant. They con-
demned by contrast the ruggedness of one
bard, who seemed like the Carthaginian hero
to make his way through philosophical mountains by the free use of vinegar which set pal-
ates on edge. They pointed the moral of the
mawkish sentimentality of another, who was
descending the wrong side of the heights he
had climbed, in the character of a lean and
slippered pantaloon. Leslie's good sense felt
that they were likely to make him ridiculous;
but all the same, that he should have been
raised to such a standard of comparison was
flattering.

"So you see, my dear old fellow, you really
are a celebrity," said Jack, who had been watching him as he ran over the pages with curious
though affectionate sympathy. "Let me make
the most of this evening, while I have you to
myself. To-morrow, when you show yourself
in Pall Mall or Paternoster Row, you will be
caught up in a chariot of fire, which will whirl
you away to the heights of Olympus, in a Milky
Way of cards of invitation."

"Confound the metaphors which you confound yourself, Jack. Seriously, I am very thankful for all this, though of course I know that all the flattery and exaggerated praise may only end in a reaction. I did think there was real stuff in the poem: so far I believe the reviewers to be in the right. In fact, everything depended on how it struck their fancy. I was treading a bridge of Al Sirat, between praise and utter perdition. The chances of the cards have turned up trumps, and so far I am inexpressibly grateful. But, between ourselves, Messrs Tonson have been hard at work in all this; and you, who have had free admission behind the scenes, must know how much humbug there may be in a seeming triumph."

"Very likely. But there is no such smoke without poetic fire; and now that the hacks of Grub Street have been sent to the knacker's yard generations ago, no publishers in London have the critics at their command. Quite the contrary: and, so far as I have heard, it is the critics who sometimes sit upon the publishers. Let us allow, for the sake of argument, you are not quite the Homer or the Dante I hailed you, nevertheless you are a poet who, under extraordinary disadvantages, as you and I know, has given brilliant promise of some day arriving at immortality. Meantime, if you only make your hay while the sun shines, you are likely to have your bread pretty thickly buttered : meantime, too, you may have the run of the drawing-rooms and din- ner-tables through the season as a lion of unrivalled pretensions and proportions : mean- time, if you were not most unhappily pre- engaged, you might make a wife of some well-tochered maiden in Mayfair."

Mr Venables spoke the truth ; nor did his sagacity and his knowledge of the world deceive him. Within a fortnight after his arrival in town, the young rhymer of Roodholm had become a notoriety. The friendly head of his publishing firm, who knew everybody worth the knowing, gave a little dinner of eight in his honour. Lord Tancred offered him the choice of any number of his Mondays, at all or any of which he hoped to have the honour of seeing our northern friend at his breakfasts. He had applications from photographers to photograph him, and when these were civilly declined, a negative of a very unflattering *carte-de-visite* of his was produced somehow, freely reproduced, and industriously paraded in the shop-windows. Nor was that all. Having been persuaded to go to a dinner given in honour of the literary guild at the Mansion House, there he met Sir Stamford Scraper. It was nothing that Sir Stamford was demonstratively cordial—that might have been expected; but Sir Stamford begged the secretary to the Resident of Sarambang to name a day for dining with him, when " he would endeavour to get some people of distinction to meet him." Naturally Sir Stamford did not speak of agreeable people, but " people of distinction." That seemed a strange anomaly; it was something like the sun-god stooping from his sphere that the chairman of a great commercial corporation should actually arrange a dinner of " people of distinction," to meet the private secretary of one of the Company's *employés*. It was a phenomenon and an ominous sign of the times, when literature was coming to the front through the crowds of the worshippers of mammon; and so Sir Stamford seemed to feel it. He overflowed

with courtesy to his celebrated guest, and yet
he was in a painfully false position. Present-
ing Leslie to Lord This or to Sir Crœsus That,
he dropped altogether the origin of their acquaintance. It was not the secretary of the
Company *in partibus* that he was entertain-
ing, but the illustrious young poet, " of whom,
of course, you have heard," the owner of a
good property in the Lothians. But when
his guests took leave, after rather a pleasant
evening, Sir Stamford laid a finger on Leslie's
arm—

" Come down into my snuggery for half an
hour, Mr Leslie. I should be very glad to
improve our acquaintance, and have a chat
over a cigar before we turn in."

Leslie had become half an oriental by virtue
of his engagement to the Company. And he
might have answered, " To hear is to obey,"
in the language of the 'Arabian Nights.' He
followed his " master " into the smoking-room,
feeling himself in an oddly inconsistent position. His magnificent host had been almost
toadying him, and yet the man had been his
benefactor, and was still his patron.

Sir Stamford felt precisely similarly, though

he approached the position from an opposite point of view. In a general way, he did not think much of poets : they seemed poor creatures, who had better be locked up at Colney Hatch, or in private lunatic asylums, if their families had the means of providing for them there. But this particular poet belonged to a peculiar species, and, in fact, appeared to be a phœnix. He was courted by peers and wealthy men; he was honoured at the Mansion-House table. Strange to say, he had a business-like head upon his shoulders, and was as much at home in figures as in hexameters. And holding him to the engagement he must be thinking of throwing up would be an advantage to the Sumatra Colonisation Company, and a credit to Sir Stamford Scraper. They did hold him, to be sure, by his attachment to Miss Moray ; but that was a thread which might snap at any instant, when a score of other girls were sure to be dragging at it. Well, if the ·secretary once deliberately decided on it, he would break away in any case ; if not, it might be well to strengthen the ground - tackle. For even if Mr Leslie still contemplated a voyage to the East, he might prefer to go in the capacity of the travelling gentleman. So Sir Stamford took the bull by the horns, and went bluntly to the point.

"I never suspected, as you may suppose," he said, awkwardly enough, "that Mr Moray, in appointing a secretary, was engaging a budding Milton. I scarcely like to suggest that you should stick to your engagement, and yet I should be extremely sorry were you to give it up. We need men of your talent in the East there; and I need not say it shall not be a trifle in the way of pecuniary arrangements that will stand against our continuing to count on your assistance."

Another man, puffed up with a new-born sense of importance, and foreseeing unexpected probabilities of filling his purse, might have resented the tone,—and Leslie was especially sensitive to any want of refinement. But he remembered that the pompous chairman had stood his friend, when the kindness that was offered had seemed all in all to him. Even now it might be much to him rejoining his love in a capacity that made him one of the family. The good wine might have had something to do with it; but he resolved to take

Sir Stamford into his confidence—and it was possibly the wisest thing he could have done.

"Perhaps you know enough of me already, Sir Stamford, to believe I shall do the best I can for you in every case. But for personal reasons, which you may possibly suspect, I am anxious to remain on the strength of your establishment. I trust that the state of my mother's health will admit of my starting for Sarambang very shortly. And if you will continue to allow me some licence about leaving, I shall beg you to say nothing as to an increase of pay. I owe you a personal debt of gratitude."

"Say no more, my dear sir; say no more!" exclaimed Sir Stamford, in great jubilation. "You are one of the men whom no success can spoil; and you are such a treasure as the Company is too happy to possess. We are friends, I hope, from this night forward: it is I, the chairman, who tell you so; and neither you nor your uncle, nor yet that very pretty cousin of yours, shall have cause to regret your candour, if I can help it."

CHAPTER XXXII.

"JACK HAS AN INSPIRATION."

WE should be doing Mr Venables injustice if
we let it be supposed that he was in any way
jealous of his friend's new-born fame. It was
very much the reverse. Jack seemed to take
Ralph's success as his own, and was never
weary of sounding his praises. He began to
correspond regularly with his cousin Grace,
telling her much that Ralph's modesty suppressed; and he enclosed many laudatory
articles from the newspapers, which the maiden
might twist if she pleased into chaplets for her
lover's brow. He insinuated delicately how,
reading between the lines, Grace might see that
Ralph was making her "famous by his pen."
"And when he joins you in that savage principality of yours," Jack went on, "he is just the
fellow, like the poetical marquis, to make you

' glorious with his sword.' Though I trust de-
voutly he may never have the chance : were it
otherwise, I should volunteer for his travelling
companion." Little did he think when he
penned these light words, that circumstances
would soon give them sinister meaning.

He wrote Moray too, and his letters to the
man of action were the complement of those
he dashed off to the young lady. Short, serious, and well considered, he dwelt upon the
poet's phenomenal success, so far as both fame
and lucre were concerned. "The better I know
him, the more I love him : he is one of those
fellows that no flattery can spoil, and of flattery he is likely to have more than enough.
To me, who know his business qualities so well,
it appears strange that any man can be so
doubly gifted—so marvellously double-sided,
if I may use the expression. Everybody in
turn is eager to make a lion of him ; but I
need hardly say his heart is not in the Highlands, but in Sumatra. When he comes out
to you, you will find him more modest than
before—ready, as he is able, to help you in
everything. Even that pompous old fool Sir
Stamford admits that his going out as a subor-

dinate is sending a razor-blade to do the work
of a jungle-axe ; but we know that the appointment is nominal and provisional ; and as for
Ralph, I need hardly say he would not ex-
change it to be Governor-General of India or
the Grand Lama.   In all sincerity, my dear
uncle, had she sought the world over, my
cousin could hardly have chosen more happily.
She will marry a man among men, and the
best of all possible husbands.   In all sincerity
I feel a double smart of sorrow and of shame,
when I remember that I once put myself forward as his rival.   But that is past and gone,
and if I am not best man at the wedding, it
will only be because, as I trust, he will soon
get married in the Indies."

No: Mr Venables was far, indeed, from
being envious.   It was amusing and almost
touching to see the friends together : Jack,
respecting Leslie for his practical qualities,
reverenced a genius which he felt to be removed above his sphere, and perhaps exaggerated the rarity of gifts to which he made
no sort of pretension ; while Ralph retained
his old honest admiration for Jack as one of
the fellows who seem born to succeed, by

energy, audacity, and fertility of resource. Besides which, in the nobility of his own nature, he did even excessive justice to Jack's undoubted generosity. Here was a youth who, though honourable and high-spirited, had never made much pretence to very lofty principles. Thinking less of the means than of the ends at which he was driving, under such training as that of the veteran Winstanley he might well have become prematurely and most selfishly worldly. Yet what had Jack's conduct been towards himself? A consistent course of self-abnegation and self-sacrifice. If Jack did owe him a life, he had paid the debt a dozen times over. He had not only given him Grace, doing the utmost in his power to forward the marriage. But what struck Ralph as almost more remarkable, Jack had laid aside the vanity and self-sufficiency which had once been his most conspicuous foibles. In their familiar relations, he had fallen so entirely into the second place, that Leslie was often positively embarrassed by the tacit flattery which was so obviously sincere. While, when they were together in public, Jack almost forgot himself, and was always pushing his modest

friend to the front, till Leslie would feel bound
to move and speak, simply that he might
escape the well-intended pressure.   In fact,
the pair were become a Pylades and Orestes,
though with none of the effusiveness of these
heroes of classical tragedy.

No : Mr Venables was so far from being
envious, that he was rather revolving like a
modest satellite round the new constellation
that had arisen above the literary horizon.
Or, to change the figure, if he was not resting
on his oars—for inaction was abhorrent to his
active nature—he had never before taken his
pulling so leisurely. And he might have taken
things as quietly for some time longer, to go
off sooner or later in one of his spurts, had it
not been for somebody who was beginning to
work upon him, though as yet he was unconscious of the influence.

Julia Winstanley was a handsome girl, and
Jack and she, as I have said, had always lived
in the utmost good-fellowship. But Jack, with
all his energy, was one of the men who feel
bound to give vent to the affections in some
shape.   He indulged in flirtations when pretty
girls crossed his path, just as he was civil to

City men on principle. But he craved for
something better and more comforting; and
when he longed for consolation after losing
Grace, he began to feel the necessity of filling
the void. It had never occurred to him to
make love to Julia Winstanley, although undoubtedly there were great temptations, and
worldly wisdom might have whispered that it
was advisable. But somehow he sought her
society more, and the opportunities presented
themselves each hour of the day; while Miss
Winstanley, who was Jack's junior by only
eighteen months, felt herself to be filling the
place of a mother to him. She had been much
pleased by his conduct at Glenconan, where he
had anticipated her wishes by offering himself
to Grace, and by placing his means and his
prospects at the disposition of Grace's father.
She had been no less pleased by the resignation with which he had let Grace go; and by
the manly firmness he had displayed in his
character of rejected admirer. And she had
appreciated, if she could not altogether understand, the generosity with which he had been
singing the praises of Leslie.

All the same, she came to the conclusion

that that sort of thing had been carried quite
far enough.   Leslie was the special property
of her friend Grace, and heaven knew that
she did not grudge the poet to the exile.   But
then Jack Venables was likewise a friend,—the
protégé in some sense of herself as well as her
father : and it seemed to her high time that
Jack should assert himself by another of those
coups which had gone so far to advance him.

Considering the direction whither their
friendship was apparently tending, it was one
of the ordinary pieces of luck of this favourite
of fortune that he should have snatched the
game out of Miss Winstanley's hands.   It is
true that it was she who gave the hint on
which he chivalrously acted, and that she
consequently came to regard his exploit as
that of a champion vowed to her service.

The hint came casually of a conversation at
a little dinner at Lord Wrekin's.   The Lord
President of the Council entertained one or
two of his illustrious colleagues, with his
brother, his sister-in-law, and their daughter.
The private secretary was there, almost as a
matter of course.   Eight people were seated at
a round table, so equally of course the conver-

sation had become general. The Ministry of
the day was, at the moment, by no means in
exuberant spirits. By-elections had been going
against them : and opposition and independent
journals alike had been arguing, with great
plausibility, that the drift of public opinion
was setting steadily against the Government
policy. In ordinary circumstances Lord Wrekin would have cared little. He was a Whig
of the ancient Whigs ; the Cabinet was far too
Radical to please him, and he would really
rather have voted any day with Lord Salis-
bury than with Lord Granville. But he clung
to his office, for he loved its dignity ; the drift
of the elections disgusted him—and he had
spoken his mind pretty strongly.

"All very true," remarked the War Minister.
"But as you know, we cannot help ourselves
in the meantime. The time for a stand may
come, meanwhile we can only temporise. But
I agree that this run of ill luck in the con-
stituencies is singularly unfortunate. There is
Ballyslattery too,—that must go to the Home-
Rulers of course : not that it greatly signifies,
since no one looks for anything else. By the
by, I ought, perhaps, to beg your pardon for

touching on the subject, since your family had so much to say to it before the Ballot Bill."

Indeed it was a sore subject with Lord Wrekin. Ballyslattery was a small seaport in Wexford county, which used to thrive *tant bien que mal* by its smuggling rather than its deep-sea fishing. The Winstanleys had considerable property in the neighbourhood; and they divided the leaseholds and the influence in the borough with the O'Geoghans, an ancient sept of the aboriginal Celts, who were likewise large landowners. By an amicable arrangement, one family and the other had always returned alternate members for the town. But the O'Geoghans had beggared themselves as the Winstanleys had grown wealthier; and in the latter times before the Land League agitation and the ballot, Ballyslattery had become pretty nearly a pocket-borough. The Winstanleys had always had to nurse and to canvass, but with canvassing and nursing they carried their man. Nowadays all that had been changed. There was a small and respectable minority of voters who bitterly regretted the old state of things. For nowadays, if you wished to give a dog—or a candidate—a bad name, you had only to send him into the streets at election time in a collar bearing Lord Wrekin's badge.

"Ay! there is Ballyslattery!" ejaculated the host, with a wry face, as if he had washed down a bad olive with a mouthful of corked Lafitte. "There is Ballyslattery, a borough that, as I may say, we made. I should be in easier circumstances to-day, Wilfred, as you know," turning to his brother, " had not our father spent a little fortune on the place. He did half the harbour-works at his own expense; he wrung a vote out of the Melbourne Cabinet, which built the breakwater, and made Bally-slattery almost a harbour of refuge. And Wilfred there, among the other irons he keeps in the fire, has been promoting lines of packets to the Bristol Channel."

"Nor have I done very badly with them," remarked Wilfred, parenthetically.

"That may be," rejoined his brother, peevishly. "Trust you for always knowing on which side to butter your bread. Anyhow, we Winstanleys have made Ballyslattery, and from being a rickle of weather-beaten hovels,

it has become a respectable and civilised town.
What is our reward ? We got it a municipal
charter, by the way, and the watchword of the
corporation is 'war to the knife' with the
family of Winstanley. The present mayor is
the very Phelim O'Callaghan, whom we had
prosecuted, fined, and imprisoned for smuggling."

"No bad reason for his being in bitter
opposition," thought Jack, though the Minister
at War was civilly sympathetic.

"The long and the short of it is, that for
the forthcoming election there are no fewer
than four candidates, and each and every one
of the four abuses me more savagely than the
others."

"Who may they be, and what are their
politics ?" inquired the mild-spoken Minister
of Public Education, who had been modestly
waiting to put in a word.

"Who are they, and what are their politics?
Why, first, to give place to rank and descent,
there is Cornelius O'Geoghan, a cadet of that
fraternity of mendicants who fights for his
own hand and for some State provision ; who
has not the faintest chance of coming in ; but

who will, nevertheless, have considerable support from out-voters in the suburban baronies.
Then there is Bodkin, the editor and pro-
prietor of the 'Ballyslattery Watchfire,' who
preaches sedition, who believes in nothing, but
who may have more or less backing from the
subscribers to his journal. There is Blake,
who believes in everything; who had a visita-
tion from the Virgin only last year; who
would revive the Inquisition, should he ever
have the chance; and who is the pet of the
bishop and the superior clergy. But the man
who will indubitably win, is an assistant-
secretary and book-keeper from the late Land
League offices in Dublin. Timothy Regan is
his confounded name : he is the son and the
pupil of a hedge-schoolmaster; he was locked
up for half a year in a lunatic ward in Swift's
hospital; he came out to stump the county of
Wexford, and to agitate behind the bars in
the Dublin public-houses. He is a *protégé* of
Parnell's; he is the darling of his fellow-
countrymen; and he will infallibly be sent up
to Westminster as a senator, to shelter behind
the privileges of Parliament, and be treated as
a gentleman by the Speaker."

The War Minister having said something commonplace and calming, discreetly let the subject drop. Lord Wrekin, remembering that he had uncourteously excited himself, was only too glad to let it go. After all, the loss of their seat of Ballyslattery was one of those irremediable evils that must be acquiesced in.

But his niece had been knitting her brows, and had gone into the drawing-room, pensive and abstracted. It was but natural that Mr Venables should be attracted to her side, seeing that they were the only two young people in the party.

"What do you think of it?" she asked, abruptly.

"Think of what?"

"Why, of this Ballyslattery election."

"What should I think of it, unless that if any Saxon wished to test the thickness of his skull, he had better be present there at the nomination or on annunciation day!"

"Oh," was all Miss Winstanley's answer; and she took to turning over a volume of etchings on which she proceeded to comment; nor did she deign one other word on the election, neither to the surprise nor the perplexity of Mr Venables.

Next morning he presented himself to his patron and official chief before the breakfast things had been cleared away.

"Are there any fresh news about the Irish election?" was his first question.

"Nothing of consequence. How should there be? Only, another candidate has come forward, professing dynamite doctrines, which will probably bring him within the clutch of the police. I have a telegram from my agent."

"Ah well, my lord, I come to propose a sixth candidate,—to ask a letter to your agent, which may be an answer to his telegram, and to beg a short leave of absence."

"No, no, my dear Mr Venables," answered his lordship, after some moments of reflection —"no, no; it will never do. You would only make a fool of yourself, and get your head broken several times over."

"With all deference to your local knowledge, and to your greater experience, I am by no means so sure of that, my lord. After what you told us last night, the conflicting

interests seem to be so many and so various,
that any one really Conservative, though he
might call himself Whig, should have a fair
chance of slipping in."

Jack paused for a moment over this ambigu-
ous profession of political faith; but Lord
Wrekin merely smiled. Member of her Majesty's Government as he was, his own opinions were not far removed from those of the
Carlton, and he felt with Jack that the days
were drawing nigh when genuine Conservatism
arrayed against Radicalism and Socialism
might meet at a great battle of Armageddon.

Jack marked the smile and went on.

"As you said last night, the candidate of
the Parnellites appears to be the only one who
is really dangerous. May I ask, by the way,
for it is of vital importance, whether your
agent has both brains and courage; whether
he is a man with pluck as well as sagacity?"

"Fitzgerald has both. I can answer for him."

"Very well; then all should be comparatively smooth sailing. We contrive to keep
the rival candidates in the field, or most of
them, which is *de bonne guerre*, and strictly
honourable as political strategy, and we fight

this seat of Ballyslattery by bringing each independent voter to the poll who dreads the
prospect of proscription and a war of races,
and objects to sending up a delegate of the
dregs of the populace."

"Whether you win or lose, you will assuredly have your head broken, my good boy."

"Forgive me if I remind you that that is
my affair. I hope my head may be patched
up before the expiration of my leave of absence. Seriously, Lord Wrekin, I believe I
can snatch the seat, and it is worth risking
something in so good a cause."

Lord Wrekin was not prepared to dispute
that proposition. After all, Jack, though a
useful secretary, was his secretary and not his
son. And had he been his son and heir, as
he told himself very nobly, he would never
have scrupled to venture him on such a for-
lorn-hope—especially had he gone fighting the
battle of the Winstanleys. If he did not give
give him his blessing, he yielded assent; he
gave him good wishes and letters of introduction; and he insisted, moreover, as matter of
business between man and man, on opening
Jack a credit with the family bankers.

CHAPTER XXXIII.

THE BATTLE OF BALLYSLATTERY.

I SHALL be brief with the Ballyslattery election, for it is but an episode, as I am aware; but then it is an episode with a bearing on the story. For Jack fought the battle less from ambition or as a political gladiator, than as the champion of a fair lady. And whether he should decide to profit by his devotion or not, his chivalrous adventure gained him both gratitude and admiration.

It only wanted five days of the nomination, and the citizens of the flourishing Wexford seaport were already in extremely warm water, fast poppling up to the boiling-point. The police had been strengthened by drafts from the surrounding districts; and two additional companies of the second battalion of the Mid-Lothian Regiment had taken up their quarters in the rambling barracks. Notwithstanding which, the playful spirit of the local politicians was breaking bounds night after night. It was breaking windows as well, as the electors suspected of constitutional leanings found to their cost; and heaven only knew what might happen. "Glory be to God!" ejaculated the corporation of the glaziers piously, rubbing their hands over incalculable reparations of damages, as the "boys" grew more boisterous. At dozens of public meetings, held day after day, agitators ranted and raved on the platforms. Morning, noon, and night, the drink was flowing at the public-houses, as if a corps of Bacchuses, come straight down from Olympus, were bestriding the casks and turning on the taps *ad libitum*.

One fine spring evening, when the excitement was nearly at its height, a traveller, as the older novelists say, might have been seen stepping out of the train at the Ballyslattery platform. Little did the car-driver who carried off the stranger, with hand-bag, hat-box, and portmanteau, after a free fight with his comrades, suspect the personality or the purposes of his fare. Otherwise our friend

Jack Venables would have been undoubtedly
"spilt" or "kilt," and very possibly both,
in place of being safely delivered at his
destination, which was the comfortable mansion of Mr Fitzgerald, Lord Wrekin's confidential agent. But though his advent was
unannounced to the town, sundry telegrams
in cipher had preceded him. Mr Fitzgerald,
who was a man of convictions as well as
courage, gave his guest the most cordial reception; but as time was precious, while con-
ducting him to the supper-table, he was already explaining what had been done.

"The presses of 'The Mercury,'—that's our
moderate Ministerial paper—have been at
work, and the address you forwarded by
message"—a special messenger had been
sent on with letters, twelve hours in advance
of the traveller—"is all ready to be quietly
posted up, as soon as the good ·people are
gone to bed. You seem to have used the
cayenne-pepper-castor pretty freely, by the
way, Mr Venables."

"Too freely, I fear, for your comfort, Mr
Fitzgerald."

"Well, so far as that goes, my foot is set

down. The dice were cast when his lordship decided to send us a candidate, and I made up my mind to stand the hazard of the die. After all, I don't know that it greatly signifies. I was hardly on a bed of roses before; and if I do multiply my enemies, it scarcely matters. We Irish agents are used to being shot at, as the eels are used to skinning. But with you, who are less in the habit of these political amenities, it is a different matter."

" It is a different matter indeed," exclaimed Jack, suspending his attack on a cold sirloin. " It is a different matter, for you will be left to bear the brunt of the animosities I provoke for a day or two, under the protection of soldiers and police. On my word, I feel like a cur that cuts in to snatch a bone, and whether he mouths it or misses it, makes a bolt with his tail between his legs."

" Faith, sir, a missile, or a charge of slugs, may reach you before you can get clear away. But as for my danger, don't speak of it again. What is your pleasure is my duty. And not to be inhospitable, when you are done with your supper, we must decide on the measures with which we shall open the campaign."

Next morning the electors of Ballyslattery were rubbing their eyes, and trying to clear away the cobwebs from whisky-sodden brains. Could it be a mirage reflected from the spirits swallowed the night before; or was it possible that a Conservative or " a bloody and brutal Whig"—practically the same thing— was come to contest the borough of Bally-slattery? There were blue and yellow posters flaunting from each wall and each street-corner; and some dirty Saxon, who dared to declare himself against Home Rule, was tampering with the freedom of Irish election.

" Sure and it's he who would have the bad chance, if the boys were to come across him," was the philosophical sentiment of a venerable patriarch who had cheered O'Con-nell and conspired with Smith O'Brien, though years had cooled his blood, spite of perpetual infusions of poteen.

" It's Fitzgarald that the boys would be daling with, —— to his sowl," remarked the more practically minded Dennis O'Dempsey, landlord of the Cat and the Bagpipes. " It's

Fitzgarald that is at the bottom of it, and by the powers——"

When Mr O'Dempsey, remembering prudence, wound up his sentence in dumb show, by a whistle and a movement of his forefinger.

These two significant ejaculations may give an idea of the state of popular feeling. The mob simply swore to murder their Saxon invader, and to take measures to picket the polling - stations against the votes of the English and the "thraitors." But as the police and "the army" were likely to make counter-demonstrations, and as some of the minority of the respectable might have resolution enough to record their votes under cover of the bayonets and the ballot, the cooler heads among the seditious met to hold council together.

" We have got five men in the field among us," said the worthy Father Dennis, who had taken Mr Blake under his especial protection, —" we have got five men in the field among us ; and, all allowances made, to say the least of it, that is two too many."

" And if your reverence is maning me," retorted Bodkin, the unbeliever, ruffling up his

plumes like a game-cock that is challenged,
" you wor never more mistaken, and it is
much to say, than when you dramed that it
was the like of me would be thinking of
withdrawing."

As for Mr Regan, as the *protégé* of Mr
Parnell, he felt confident of the place he was
competing for, and had already discounted the
pay, in bright visions of the imagination.
While the remaining candidates, knowing well
in their hearts that they had no chance, determined to put spokes in the wheels of their
enemies.

The council was composed of the *prud'-
hommes* of the place: it embodied all the
virtue and the wisdom of local patriotism.
And the upshot of their proceedings was
embodied in a resolution, moved by Mr
O'Teague, a student of the Cork College, and
one of the most fervid expositors of the advanced ideas of Young Ireland,—

" As this Mr Venables has come among us—
and may the divil recaive his sowl !—as if he
wor expectin' that we would be prowd and
happy to return him, I am of opinion that
we should show our sensibility to his poloite-

ness by giving him another competitor to compate with. It's myself that will issue an address to the free and independent electors, and now he will have five of us to fight with in place of four."

And O'Teague stuck to his logical determination. Strange to say, he gathered a considerable tail of supporters, who applauded the sagacious stroke of patriotism to the echo. If Jack Venables had paid him — and his enemies swore afterwards that he had done so —O'Teague could not have more effectually played into his hands.

The nomination day was a great day in Ballyslattery. The population had been in a state of chronic intoxication for a week before; but the spirits had boiled their blood without sapping their physical energies. The authorities had made formidable preparations. There was an immense force of police, mounted and on foot. The Mid-Lothian Regiment was strategically distributed, so as to take up commanding positions where they were free to act; while sundry troops of the Lancers formed in sections of equestrian statues in certain open spaces. But on the other hand, the back streets

and the tortuous lanes of the town were given
over to gangs of the "boys." Bands of sturdy
rustics, drafted from the country districts for
the occasion, were marshalled under local leaders with their "slips of blackthorns" in their
fists. The amphibious population of fisher-
men, with many seafaring sympathisers, had
come ashore. Some of them were armed with
cudgels or boat-stretchers; not a few with improvised pikes or with cutlasses. The hobbledehoys of the alleys mustered strong in their
wake; while behind the hobbledehoys came
the school-urchins, with their pockets or their
waist-bands so many small arsenals of stones,
and skilled, like David, in slinging and stone-
throwing. And all these were waiting for the
proceedings to begin, that they might claim
their due shares in the ceremony.

It might have all seemed very natural to a
native-born Wexford man; but it struck a
stranger as peculiar. So, perhaps, we may as
well quote a passage or two from the Venables
correspondence; for, according to promise,
Jack dashed off hasty despatches each night
to his friend Ralph Leslie as well as to Miss
Winstanley.

The latter were perhaps the more confidential as to his innermost feelings; but as the former were more frank as to the perils which he faced, we shall fall back upon them in preference.

"DEAR RALPH,—   .   .   .

"You have never been cast away and shipwrecked as I have been. Worse luck for you and me, for in that case I might have spared you a detailed description of the nomination scene. You have never heard the wild winds howling and shrieking through shrouds and stays, while the roaring breakers were chafing against the shore—with, by the by, the bellowing of a deck-load of maddened cattle thrown in by way of aggravation! I assure you, when I made my appearance in the streets, before the hour of noon the day before yesterday, I was carried back in the spirit to the 'Kittiewake's Neb.' The procession of the Ministerialist candidate was very like a tadpole—with a head, little body, and a great deal of tail. Fitzgerald and a few stanch gentlemen and people of business stood by me like men. More credit to them, for I fear they

may smart sorely for it. Most folks who had
any decent excuses sent them instead of coming. Small blame to them. We were preceded, not by a band, but by a strong body of
police. Mounted policemen mustered on each
side of us; and another small cohort of blue-
coated footmen brought up the rear. Each
open space was occupied by troops, hemmed in
by mixed mobs of ruffians, with their Megæra-
like women and their squalling brats.

"The yelling, hooting, cursing, the cries of
grief and hate, might have been heard to any
imaginable distance. Appius Claudius, or
Warren Hastings under the blighting invec-
tive of Burke, could hardly have shrunk —
morally—more pitiably than I did. To be
sure there were occasional showers of stones,
coming by way of distraction from the execra-
tions and blasphemies. But I was braced by
the very audacity of the abuse and assaults,
and 'Richard was himself again,' when I stood
forward upon the platform. It was just as
well, for even Wirtz or Gustave Doré, in their
nightmares of inspiration, could hardly conceive more fiendlike forms than those before
which we found ourselves. My opponents

snapped and snarled among themselves; but it was for me, and more especially for poor Fitzgerald, they reserved the most venomous atrocities and the gnashing of their teeth.

"You may fancy I might have been stunned and muzzled. Quite the contrary. You have no idea how easy it is being eloquent under such circumstances. Had I routed through the horn of a wild bull on the platform, the sound would never have reached the second ranks in the crowd. I merely moved my lips and stooped towards the reporter at my elbow, ducking occasionally to dodge a stone or a dead cat. The reporter, sitting under an umbrella quilted with tin plates, pretended to lend an ear, and made fictitious play with his pencil. He had my eloquence cut and dry in his pocket, and had already telegraphed it. It will appear at length in the Ministerial journals of Dublin, and will be strained down into paragraphs for the letters to the London press. . . . I understand something of the feelings of the first of the martyrs, and await anxiously and in strict seclusion the declaration of the poll."

A second extract from a letter, bearing date two days subsequently :—

"It was pretty warm with us, as you may remember, on the nomination ; but the fires were seven times heated for the declaration of the poll. When you saw by telegram that I had snatched a scratch victory by three votes, you may have formed a conception of the popular reception of the result. But in this Irish atmosphere one comes to be acclimated to blasphemies. The mixed multitude of savages before the hustings cast all self-control to the winds. Decently dressed men, farmers in frieze coats, and shopkeepers in broadcloth, like those whose rags were skewered on to them by a single pin, seemed to be alike possessed by legions of demons. Had it not been for the muster of the soldiers and the police, they would have joined their friends on the platform with a rush, and torn me and my handful of backers into ribbons. Still, happily for us, they deemed discretion the better part of valour ; and it is strange, indeed, that the Celts, with their personal pluck, should lose heart in a crowd like so many curs that are collared. To be sure, after a time of howling, they warmed up into action, and a corps of rapscallions made an aggressive demonstration. Police and soldiers were half paralysed; for, as no magistrate had cared to read the Riot Act, they did not choose to use carbines and revolvers.   Then I remarked the beauty of the weapons of the Lancers as comparatively harmless arms for repressing a Hibernian riot. The men charged in loose formation with the lance; their assailants took refuge under the upturned carts and handbarrows that filled the market-place.   They were poked and thrust at good-humouredly enough, considering the provocation they had offered to the troopers— many of whom had been bruised and battered by the stones.   Then—will you believe it?— this extraordinary people, who had been like unchained savages only the minute before, began to laugh and recover their good-humour, as if they had been pleasantly tickled by the points of the lances.   I fancy it is the sort of fun that comes home to them; and there is more delicacy in such repartees than in the blows of their blackthorn cudgels. . . . At all events, I come back to you the member for Ballyslattery; and assuredly there was no cor-

ruption to unseat me, though there may have
been something approaching to intimidation
on the other side; and as I have not the
faintest prospect of re-election, no possible
pressure from my constituents can influence
my parliamentary action. I am only sorry for
poor Fitzgerald, who has stood by me like a
brick. But what can I, or what, indeed, can
Lord Wrekin, do for him, unless his lordship
gave him his dismissal with a pension? and
then he would never consent to expatriate
himself. Neither you nor I had any idea,
my dear Ralph, of what the men must resign
themselves to who stand in the breach between the English garrison and the disloyalists
who beleaguer it."

Jack hurried back to town, bearing his
blushing honours, as well as sundry bruises
he had received in the flying storms of stones.
He took his departure by a late train on the
very day of the declaration of the poll. He
was loath to seem to leave Fitzgerald in the
lurch; but that gentleman sensibly pointed
out that his going might possibly allay popular excitement, while his remaining would
certainly excite it to madness. So our tri-

umphant young friend was escorted to the
train by a serried phalanx of police and a
couple of squadrons of cavalry. "Had I been
the Pope or the Sultan, they could not have
treated me with greater distinction," he remarked, as, following portmanteau and hand-
bag, he passed between the triple ranks of
the gallant Mid-Lothian men, drawn up to
right and left before the station. And even
higher honours were in store for him, as he
learned later. That night his constituents,
with the non-electors, rose almost *en masse*
to burn their new member in effigy; and on
the following Sunday he was solemnly cursed
with book, bell, and candle, from half the
altars in the diocese of Ballyslattery.

CHAPTER XXXIV.

STARTLING INTELLIGENCE FROM SANGA.

THE managing director or Resident of the
Sumatra Company at Sanga had, on the whole,
a pleasant voyage to Penang. He had started
in considerable ignorance of the territory he
was sent to administer, though he knew a
good deal about the trade he was to direct.
But his Company had furnished him with
ample materials to study, and these he had
supplemented by a travelling library, which
was well selected, if small. Reading early and
late, and in his perpetual intervals of leisure,
he had primed himself as to the facts that
concerned him ; and he communicated the
information he acquired to his daughter, who
was naturally curious as to the future to which
they had hopefully committed themselves.

I have no idea of boring my readers with

the facts, the fallacies, and the statistics to which Grace, like Desdemona, seriously inclined her ear. Briefly, the broad district of Sanga had been transferred to the Company by the Sultan of Sarambang. Sarambang is a wild state in Sumatra, lying nearly opposite to Perak, in the Malay Peninsula. To the north and west is the independent State of Achin; to the south and the east are the lands of sundry savage races under the shadowy suzerainty of the kingdom of Holland. According to a Malay proverb, which we venture to translate freely into our vernacular, Kulong Hassim, Sultan of Sarambang, found himself between the devil and the deep sea. The pirate fleets of the Achinese were ravaging his coasts, carrying women and children into captivity. Not that there was a pin to choose between the Achinese and the Sarambangese; but his people, being the weaker, were being pushed to the wall. While, on the other hand, being cute, he shrewdly suspected that it might occur to the Dutch to champion his cause, whether he would or not. In which case, whoever might swallow the oyster, it was pretty sure he would be left with nothing but the shells. In those circumstances, he had listened willingly to an English adventurer, who had come to Sarambang ostensibly for shooting. His district of Sanga lay remote to the south, and its shores were being perpetually swept by descents of piratical Dyaks. He must either defend it or give it up. As he could not do the former, he decided on the latter, more especially as Colonel Chamberlain made him a tempting offer. The Sultan practically sold an indefinite liferent of a district geographically defined by certain rivers, and carrying a scattered population of over 100,000 souls. The stipulated price was a trifle of money down, with a moderate royalty on all the profits which the English settlers might realise. Chamberlain's bargain was speculative but good; nor was the bargain by any means bad for the Sultan. Anything he might subsequently make of the contract was so much clear gain; and the politic Chamberlain had really made him a sleeping partner, with a heavy stake in the prosperity of the foreign settlers. If Kulong Hassim could do little to help them, at all events he would show them something more than a benevolent neutrality.

Colonel Chamberlain brought his concession to London, where he finally came to terms about it with Sir Stamford Scraper. The hopes he flashed before the eyes of the promoter were dazzling; for he spoke of coal-fields and the precious metals, and unlimited crops of spices, sugar, coffee, and cotton. What with his plausibility, what with the specimens he showed, what with reference to geographical authorities, and to travellers who had written of the Malay Peninsula, he had little difficulty in making his bargain with Sir Stamford; the rather that he took the money he stipulated for in paid-up shares, making it a *sine qua non* that he was to be appointed managing director. I may say at once that I should hardly call Chamberlain an enthusiast; since there could be no question as to the intrinsic value of his concession. The doubt was, whether the English company could *exploiter* it, owing to the unsettled condition of those seas and their coasts. However, there was a precedent in Rajah Brooke's success at Sarawak. There was good fighting material among the Malays within the bounds of Sanga, who would rejoice in the security from aggression that might be given by a strong government; and on that Colonel Chamberlain pinned his faith. Though more of a sportsman and speculator than an administrator, he had discharged his unfamiliar responsibilities fairly well. He had founded the settlement of Sanga on the Sanga river, and fortified it with stockades; he had imported a few skilled European artisans, one or two capable clerks to keep his accounts, and sundry respectable non - commissioned officers to drill his coffee-coloured levies. He had begun to open up and develop his resources; he had fought sundry piratical fleets, and succeeded in beating them off; he had been habituating his Malay subjects to the pleasures of working for regular pay; and he had seen a steamer — the Sir Stamford Scraper—sent out to him, which might ply between the settlement and Penang or other ports. Finally, the unlucky Chamberlain had caught a fever and died, in the nick of time for any interest in my story, just as Glenconan with his fortunes seemed to have been cast hopelessly adrift.

So Glenconan and his daughter had had an agreeable passage, and they had transhipped themselves at Penang to the Sir Stamford Scraper, which had come thither by appointment to meet the Resident.

The curtain that dropped on Grace falling back in a faint on the deck of the Fire King in the fogs from the Essex marshes, rises on her as she is approaching Sanga and the shores of the promised land. The rise of the curtain was the literal fact, for there is little difference between fog and fog, whether it hangs on the lower reaches of the Thames or over the mangrove-swamps of Sumatra. But what suddenness in the difference when the southern sun breaks out! It is the broad blaze of the balefire on some Border height, to the flickering of a farthing candle in a cellar in the Seven Dials. Let Miss Grace tell her own story, as Mr Venables has done. I quote from a five-sheet letter to Miss Winstanley.

" It was with a sinking and a saddening of the heart I came on deck a little after dawn. Creeping, clinging vapours enveloped everything, weighing down the black smoke from the funnel of the steamer. It was a dimness that might be felt and almost tasted, for it came with the breath of mud and malaria and decaying vegetable matters. Shall I say, that when the steward threw a little glass of cognac into the coffee, I swallowed it as I have smelled a scent-bottle in a crowded church?

"Then, of a sudden, the grey vapours began to thin, wreathing themselves round the masts and the yards, and coming down on our heads in a drizzle; while away to the eastward was a flashing of rosy lights, like the flashes of the aurora borealis through the grimmest of wintry skies. Almost before I could rub my eyes over the phenomenon, the rosy reflections that had been radiating like revolving lights had widened into one deep, broad blaze of crimson. The sun of the tropics had broken out in his strength, and the mists melted away or evaporated as by enchantment. The mouth of the Sanga river lay before us, with the surf breaking over the troubled bar; and the smooth, heaving swell of the black channels, lying between the surge of the snow-drifts. To right and left were the thickets of mangroves, casting their gloomy shadows over sand-banks and mud-flats. But behind were the copses of feathery palms, and the clusters of the graceful bamboo columns, bending beneath the burdens of their glossy coronets of leaves. While behind all, and in the distance, was the wooded amphitheatre of mountains, their heads and shoulders rising in volcanic nakedness out of the flowing draperies of the forests that fell from their stony girdles in folds of green. I cannot help being romantic and poetical, my dear Julia, for never surely did mortal maiden look on a more glorious panorama.

"But to come back to the prosaic from the poetical, a steam - launch was puffing and wheezing alongside, in place of one of those most picturesque prahus, which seem to embody the very melody of motion. Perhaps we crossed the bar all the more easily, and we steamed up the sluggish stream very comfortably. To adopt a simile of Sir Walter Scott's, it was like threading an interminable aisle, under the leafy roof of one of the grandest of natural cathedrals. Long rows and groups of graceful columns shot up on either bank—the stems of trees that were absolutely branchless to the height of 80 or 100 feet. Then indeed in their exuberance they made up for lost time, interlacing themselves in impenetrable arches of foliage, the light filtering through at intervals, as from a roof in disrepair, and falling in light shreds and patches on the black surface of the stream. But the silence of that tropical forest was death-like. There might have been beasts or birds : I saw not a single one, except here and there a solitary stork that went floating skywards from his fishing-ground. There were butterflies indeed, fluttering over the launch's deck, though bats or moths might have seemed more appropriate to that twilight. Now and again we met one of the Malay boats, the rowers crooning a melancholy song, as they bent mechanically to the oars. And once there came a scream out of the depths of the forest, that jarred my overstrung nerves, so that I almost felt inclined to re-echo it; so you may imagine how far gone I must have been in my romance. They said it was some hapless fruit-eating animal being crunched in the jaws of some beast of prey. Anyhow, I felt as if the darkness had entered into my soul; as if I had been sentenced to imprisonment in a tropical dungeon. Nor could I help clutching my father's hand, though even then I was ashamed of myself,

when he soothed my terrors instead of laugh-
ing at them.

"'Wait and be patient, Grace,' was all he
said; and if I tried to follow the advice, I was
soon rewarded.

.   .   .   .   .   .

"You cannot imagine what a delightful
home is ours. The architecture would as-
tonish you in England, but it is admirably
adapted to the climate. Conjure up your
fancies of a big bungalow in the most graceful
harmonies of subdued colouring, with everything, both within and without, that is most
coquettish. It is the glorification of the useful and ornamental bamboo, which, as school-
books would say, is pretty much to the Malay
what the camel is to the Arab, or the reindeer
to the Laplander. The walls are of double
bamboo stems, interlaced and interwoven by
bamboo cordage. The partitions and the
hangings of the rooms are of bamboo matting. Mats of the softest bamboo fibre cover
the bamboo floors. And the open roof above
the bamboo rafters is of shingles cut from the
bamboo stems. Finally, my father smokes a
pipe of bamboo; the water-pitcher in the

pantry, and—for aught I know—the pots and pans in the kitchen, are made of plugged joints of the bamboo; and the beds and chairs in the broad verandahs, where we sleep and shelter through the day from the sunshine, are of that everlasting bamboo, like all the rest.

"As for the Malays, I like, nay, I love them. Every man is a gentleman, as every woman is a lady.

"I forgot to mention, by the way, that there are a few thorns among the roses. When I light the lamps, and draw the mats aside before the windows of a night, to look out on the glorious heavens, that are studded with constellations as thickly as any duchess's stomacher with the family diamonds at a drawing-room, I am smothered in a plague of most magnificent moths, that extinguish the lights in a general incremation. I shook a scorpion the other morning out of my slipper: happily I was drowsy, and the slipper slipped through my fingers, otherwise the scorpion must certainly have stung me. He was caught and crushed, which is more than I can say for a huge hairy spider, standing

about half a hand high at the shoulder, and
casting a ghastly shadow of a foot or so behind him. While I stood still and screamed,
he made off to his hole, and ever since I have
been expecting his reappearance. Then there
is a snake in the thatch just above my pillow :
I can hear him rustling there in the watches
of the night. He is supposed to be venomous; but the servants say there is no danger,
so long as there are plenty of rats and mice.
And rats and mice run about in such abundance, that even papa is not uneasy; and
thinks it better the snake should not be dis-
turbed, on account of the sentiment or religious principles of the natives — I am not
quite sure which. Nevertheless it *is* a delightful country; and if you only saw the
flowers in our garden—flowers growing wild,
for there are few under the shade of the
forests — you would be content to put up
with the snakes, and even compound for the
spiders."

In fact, Miss Moray saw most things
through rose - coloured glasses in the meantime, and so far her letters were doubly
welcome to her friends at home.

Those from Moray were likewise satisfactory
on the whole, though written rather in pen
and ink than in rose tints. He knew the
tropics so well, that they had no longer
power to interest him; and he judged the
situation in Sumatra like a man of business.
So far as he saw, the settlement was nearly
as rich in resources as it had been represented,
but much remained to be done before the
Company could reckon upon dividends as on
the Three per cents. He did every justice to
the energy and abilities of his predecessor;
but since the death of Colonel Chamberlain,
Sanga had been unsettled and retrograding.
The Dutch had been making overtures to the
Sultan of Sarambang: so far as he could
learn, the Sultan stood firm; but intrigues
had been fomented at the Court, and it was
rumoured that emissaries of the disaffected
had been already stirring up sedition in the
settlement. He apprehended no serious consequences, as the Dutch, having no shadow of
a legal claim, were not likely openly to show
their game; and agitators who fell into his
hands would be summarily dealt with. In
the meantime, the Company might count on

his being upon his guard, and he hoped to send them more reassuring intelligence very speedily.

It need hardly be said that those despatches, worded as they were, made Leslie more eager than ever to join his uncle. There was madness in the thought of Grace in those Malay jungles, exposed to the chance of intrigue and savage warfare, and leaning in her isolation on the single life of a man whose duties must necessarily expose him to danger. Yet leaving England was out of the question, so long as his mother hung between life and death. Mrs Leslie had been making encouraging progress, it was true; but any cause of anxiety might have the most serious consequences.

That knot was cut when he least expected it. He had left his mother fairly strong and in unusually good spirits, for one of his flying trips to the south. Two days afterwards a letter reached him, to say that all was over. The event had been so sudden, from an affection of the heart, that on this occasion there was no need to shock him by telegraphing. Ralph had hurried home to superintend the arrangements for the funeral; and morbidly

self-reproachful for his undutiful impatience
to be away, he had been smarting under a
double sense of suffering.   He had seen his
mother laid in her grave ; he had sent away
his friends ; he had dined *tête-à-tête* with the
relative who had nursed Mrs Leslie through
her illness ; and then had withdrawn to the
solitude of his own room to pass a melancholy
evening.   A pile of unopened papers lay upon
a table : he opened the one that first came to
hand, in sheer distraction of spirits.   It chanced
to be a London evening journal, and he ran
his eye unconcernedly down the middle pages.
His eye was caught by a telegram, headed
" Penang," and dated a couple of days
before.   It was brief enough and bitter
enough :—

" There are rumours, which, however, want
confirmation, of an attack by the independent
and piratical tribes on the settlement of the
Sumatra Company at Sanga.   It is said that
the managing director has been killed, and the
settlement carried by storm.   As the Company's steamer has been sent hither for
repairs, we may have no certain intelligence
for some weeks.   Meantime, we may repeat

that the intelligence must be received with caution."

There was nothing that Ralph had studied more regularly of late than the time-tables of the P. & O. Steam Navigation Company. He never knew when a piece of knowledge might be of use. " Thank God !" he ejaculated, " if I start to-morrow morning, I can catch the next packet for the Straits from Brindisi."

CHAPTER XXXV.

LESLIE LISTENS TO A CONFESSION.

PROVERBS will prove true in more senses than
one. That of " More haste, less speed," would
come into Ralph Leslie's head when the " Flying Scotchman " ran itself into some goods
waggons and off the rails, just before entering
Darlington Station. It had been " slowing,"
and so no great damage was done ; but there
was delay in the delivery of the passengers
in London. So Ralph " missed connections "
with the South-Eastern train, and consequently
with the steamer he hoped to catch at Brindisi. It was not in his nature to tear his
hair or rend his garments ; but none the less
was he miserable and bitterly disappointed.
He did the best and wisest thing in the circumstances, and had himself driven to the
Sumatra offices in Leadenhall Street. There

he found no less a person than Sir Stamford
Scraper. For the calming of their shareholders, the Board had sent a circular to all
the City editors, stating that they had received
no unsatisfactory news from the Settlement,
and intimating that they saw no reason to attach
the slightest importance to the alarming re-
ports which had been rashly set afloat. Nevertheless, though the chairman tried to put a
pleasant face upon it, it was evident that he
was anxious, not to say alarmed. Of course
his anxiety communicated itself to Leslie, whose
poetic imagination had perhaps got the better
of his common-sense, and was conjuring up
every kind of appalling tragedy. Before the
lover and the chairman had talked together for
ten minutes, they had almost frightened each
other into temporary fits, though Leslie was
in the deepest mourning. On the principle,
possibly, of never crying over spilt milk, Sir
Stamford had uttered no syllable of condolence
as to the death of his visitor's mother; and
in the horror of the bereavements which were
still in suspense, Leslie had not resented or
even remarked the omission.

"So you are going out at last, Mr Leslie,"

exclaimed Sir Stamford. "I am delighted to hear it. Even should all be well, we are short-handed at Sanga; or rather, we are short-headed. And should anything have happened——"

There Leslie made a gesture that interrupted him. "Well, well, we will hope the best; and I don't attach any importance to the telegram. But you have missed the Candahar at Brindisi—there can be no question of that."

"No question whatever; and now, how to get on. To tell the truth, that was what brought me here so quickly: I thought your people might be able to inform me."

"To be sure—to be sure; our manager is the very man. He has all the sailings and the steamings for the Straits at his finger-ends."

And Sir Stamford, ringing the bell, sent a message, begging Mr Jennings to step that way. The accuracy of Mr Jennings's information did not belie his character.

"If you have missed the Candahar, Mr Leslie, it does not much matter. That is to say, if, by way of consolation for roughish

fare and some lack of society, you can content yourself with tolerable speed and plenty
of space—— You don't care about such
trifles? Ah, very well; then I have your
affair all ready managed for you. You
know, sir," he said, turning to the chairman,
"Brooks, Bateson, & Co. will be ready to do
anything for us,—as they well may, for we
are their best customers. Their steamer, the
Canton Castle, ought to touch at Palermo
three days hence. She has swift despatch
for Palermo, Port Said, Penang, and Singapore. Starting this evening and travelling
straight on, Mr Leslie can easily be in Sicily
to meet her, unless there should be a hitch
in communications from Naples. But with
your permission, sir, I can easily settle with
the owners to send a message to their agents
at Palermo. There the ship will be detained
over her lading till Mr Leslie turns up."

"Do so, Mr Jennings; do so by all means
—that is to say, if you are agreeable, Mr
Leslie. And remember, when you get out
to Sanga, should anything have happened
to the Resident, that you are to spare no
expense in forwarding news by special vessels

or otherwise; and I may as well give you a written authority to that effect."

"If anything should have happened to the Resident!" thought Ralph, as he was driven westward again to the office of the President of the Council, where he hoped to find Jack Venables. It was clear that those shrewd men of business in Leadenhall Street feared the worst, although they were trying to hope the best. And what a journey lay before him, to be travelled out in the thickening horrors of suspense! Under any circumstances, he could hope to hear nothing until his steamer communicated with the shore at Port Said.

Jack Venables, with his many irons in the fire, had always been a doubtful bargain to the Government: though doing his official work by fits and starts, his spurts were often worth the plodding routine of other men. Now that he was to sit in the House for Ballyslattery, he had given in his resignation to his noble friend and patron, and was only filling his official arm-chair until his successor should be appointed. So it was with even an easier conscience than usual that he had hustled all the bundles of papers aside, and bade the messenger deny him to everybody whose business was not absolutely urgent. His body was there within the precincts of the Council office,—worse luck,— but his thoughts were far away in the spice-groves of the Southern Pacific.

"My dear Leslie—my dear Ralph, I had been looking for you to-morrow, but hardly to-day."

Ralph blushed at what seemed a hinted accusation of heartlessness, though Jack had never meant it so. Taking a misfortune in Sumatra, or the probability of some misfortune, for granted, he rapidly ran over what he had been doing, and told what he had arranged. "My traps have been all ready for long; there is no difficulty about them. I leave the heavy luggage to be sent out after me; and I start for Naples in light travelling equipment, with a rifle, a carbine, and a couple of revolvers besides. Surely it was by some presentiment that I provided myself with so formidable a battery."

"But, God bless me, Ralph!" said Jack, smiling sadly, "you know you never could hit a hay-stack!"

"And I hardly profess to be a crack shot now. But all the same, I have been making progress. I have been practising steadily with pistols, and with the rifle at the volunteer range near Roodholm. And you know I am pretty cool, and have my nerves under tolerable command, as some of those Malays may learn on occasion," he went on, with such a look as Jack had never seen before on his placid and handsome features.

"Heaven help us! after all, he is but one of ourselves," thought Jack; "and I, for one, should be sorry to face him, if he were thirsting for *my* blood and *his* were up."

The next idea that occurred to him, as it had occurred before, was that he would cast his constituents and his City affairs to the winds, and be off with Ralph that very evening. There were historical precedents in favour of such prompt action. Had not Lord Clyde gone off to take the command in India with something like a half-dozen of collars and a tooth-brush? and he flattered himself that he was better provided. But the calmer Ralph had no idea of letting his friend play the fool in performing the Pylades to his Orestes.

"My path of duty is plain, and it leads me straight to the Canton Castle at Palermo. You have nothing to do on board that *galère*; and permit me to add, that should you leave England suddenly, you would be behaving badly to many of the people you left behind."

"Possibly you are right," sighed Jack, reluctantly giving up his wild proposal. "If the worst comes to the worst, you can always telegraph for me, though it takes time going half across the globe. What fun you may have in the way of fighting! No, I don't mean that; but it is hard to be doomed to sit with my hands crossed while you go to the help of our friends, should they need help."

"God knows, you need not envy me the voyage," was the reply; "and my time of involuntary inaction will be intolerable torment."

In answer to which, the only comfort Jack could offer was a silent shaking of the hand.

Mr Jennings's predictions as to the society on board the Canton Castle were fulfilled. With the exception of a Sicilian lady, shipped for Port Said, who was chronically sea-sick, Ralph found but a single companion. As for the skipper, he was an honest old sea-dog, who seldom opened his mouth, except to give orders, or to stow away a heavy ground cargo of the rough though plentiful fare. At any other time Ralph's fellow-traveller would have greatly excited his curiosity. There was a mystery about the man, as Ralph felt from the first; but at that moment all the world was indifferent to him. He scarcely saw the precipices of the Monte Pellegrino; "The Golden Shell" glittered unheeded before his dreamy eyes; and as they steamed southwards through the glorious Straits of Messina, the Canton Castle might have been threading the icebergs of Smith's Sound, for anything Ralph knew to the contrary. Then disappointment followed disappointment. No news at Malta, where they lay broiling and unlading for a few hours; not a single word from Sumatra at Port Said; not a word at Suez. There was a hot blast from the deserts as they steamed down the Red Sea; and perhaps it rather did Ralph good than otherwise. It acted on him as an anodyne, and soothed his sharper pangs.

But it affected his fellow-traveller more seriously. Ralph and this Mr Smith had been good friends enough.   Many times in the day they exchanged ordinary civilities ; but they sat at meals in a Pythagorean silence which was seldom interrupted.   Had Captain Benbow been of a more convivial temperament, he must have cursed the fate which had given him such dull companions. Had he had the slightest sense of humour, he must have smiled, nevertheless, at the dexterity with which they cut down the table and cabin talk to the lowest point compatible with bare civility.   But as Benbow was neither convivial nor observant, he simply contented himself with wondering how two well-grown men continued to support nature on such inadequate sustenance.   Leslie looked as if he were going into a consumption, with the hectic flush on his cheeks and the wandering lights in his eyes ; while Mr Smith appeared to have gone into a decline many months before, and to be holding on to his life by something like spasms of volition.

Such being the case, it was hardly to be wondered at that Smith should have collapsed under the heat of the Red Sea ; and Leslie, for one, was not at all surprised when he

learned that the other passenger was laid up
in his cabin. The news did not shock him,
and rather did him good. It was not in his
nature to know that a fellow-creature needed
his services, without doing his best as consoler
or sick-nurse. So, rousing himself, he shook
some of his personal troubles from his shoulders, and after knocking repeatedly without
receiving a reply, he opened the door of Mr
Smith's cabin.

A glance was sufficient to show that he need
not stand upon ceremony. As the French put
it expressively, Smith was "beating the country,"—that is to say, he was tossing restlessly
in bed, and throwing his arms about in the
air, while his lips were moving and murmur-
ing inarticulately. That the case was grave
was very certain, and the Canton Castle
carried no doctor. Leslie did not gain much
by calling the skipper into consultation. Benbow prescribed a stiff brimmer of brandy-
and-water by way of specific, which did not
altogether recommend itself to Leslie's good
sense ; and the first officer mournfully shook
his head, muttering something about a sheet,
the sail-maker, and the Church-service. So

that Ralph, though he knew next to nothing of medicine, took the case into his own hands. He had the patient carried on to the deck upon a mattress, and stretched on the poop under the sail that had been rigged by way of awning. We need not go into the details of his unscientific treatment, but by indefatigable nursing he pulled the patient through.

In ordinary circumstances the success that had crowned his self - sacrifice would have richly rewarded him for his good-nature and Christian charity. So it did in a measure. Yet, all-Christian as he was, he felt something like the surgeon who has brought back to life the body of a murderer handed over to the school for anatomical purposes. In the ravings of delirium, through the watches of the night, his patient had spoken wildly and incoherently. Ralph, who had listened involuntarily and much against the grain, had nevertheless as involuntarily tried to put together the pieces of the puzzle. In that he had failed; yet he had come to the conclusion that the object of his cares must be a consummate scoundrel. And from what Ralph could gather—and it was confirmed by Smith's appearance—he had been guilty of no such daring atrocity as murder, but of swindling, a breach of trust, or forgery, or some similar scandalous felony of the first order. The only point in his favour was, that apparently remorse had been lying heavily on him.

Had Jack Venables been in Ralph Leslie's place, he would probably have been just as good-natured in the way of sick-nursing. But when Jack had revived the rascal, he would have shrunk from pressing himself as father-confessor; he would simply have declined any thanks, and cut further acquaintance. But unless I have made a poor hand of my portrait of Ralph, it will be understood that it was altogether foreign to his character that he should behave so. His good offices had pledged him to this dubious *protégé*, and conscience told him that the cure of the soul was of infinitely more consequence than the care of the body. But now that the convalescent was regaining strength, he was not to be brought to confession save of his own free will. Ralph was in more than two minds as to the depth of his patient's penitence : in any case, the chances would be in his favour if he struck while the iron was hot and made more malleable by recent affliction.

He made up his mind one evening during supper, and the opportunity came that very night. "How beautiful is night!" sighs out Thalaba in Southey's poem; and that night, undoubtedly, was most beautiful, according to an Arab's notions. The lustrous moon was riding in a cloudless sky, amid a gorgeous illumination of constellations. So brilliant was the night, that Leslie fancied he could see the flickering of the heated air between the sea and the starshine. The surface of that stirless water was broken by phosphorescent flashes, and the waves in the wake of the screw were lighted up as by myriads of wax candles, or rather by an electrical glare, for there was something "uncanny" in the radiance. With an easy mind, the weird beauties of the night would have stirred Leslie's poetical soul to its depths : as it was, his preoccupations and his dramatic instincts interested him in a solitary human personality. Smith had been making steady progress; yet now he sat huddled up in an attitude of profound dejection. If he saw the sea or the skies, he seemed to

take as little note of one or the other as a
new-born babe. "Now is my time," thought
Leslie, as he left the shadows of the funnel.
Sorely against his will he was going to discharge an imperative duty: were Smith to
meet his advances with a rebuff, it could not
touch him in anything but his vanity; yet
somehow his heart beat at double time, as if
he were bracing himself for the most moment-
ous of interviews. At the sound of the foot-
steps in the stillness of the night, Smith started like the skulking thief who feels a hand
suddenly on his shoulder. But when he saw
who it was, he quickly recovered himself,
though Ralph could fancy that he brushed
away a tear.

Mastering his instinctive repugnance, mur-
muring to himself, "May Heaven forgive me
if I am hypocritical!" he sat down by Smith's
side. The other shrank away, glanced hurriedly around him, and then sidled up, though still
shrinkingly, against Ralph, as a much-badgered
cat responds to a caress. To Ralph, whose faculties were all upon the stretch, Smith seemed
to be craving for some human fellowship, which
had long been denied him. So Ralph snatched

at the ball on the bound, and laid a gentle hand on that of the other man.

"May God bless you, Mr Leslie!" was the unexpected answer. "I may think I owe you little kindness for saving my life, but you meant well; and you have bound me to you, body and soul."

"I did what I should have done for anybody in similar case, and, so far, you owe me nothing. But if you really feel grateful, as you say, Mr Smith—and I don't doubt it—shall I tell you how you may discharge the debt?"

"Surely."

"By doubling it. There is something weighing on your mind, and you would be easier were you to make a clean breast of it."

"What! I have been talking in my delirium. I thought as much," interrupted Smith hastily, looking round him as if he would have been only too glad to bolt, had he been anywhere but on a ship in a waste of water.

"You have been talking, Mr Smith, but I have no wish to entrap you. I know nothing more of you or of your story, except that you *have* a story which you have reasons for not telling. As for me, I need not say to a man of your penetration that I am by no means curious. It is less than nothing to me personally whether you speak or not."

Smith relapsed into reflection. Ralph stirred him up, after a minute.

"I may hint, too, that since your illness and your convalescence, you have neglected certain precautions you took before. You strike me as being an older man by some fifteen years; and the illness, though it has pulled you down, does not account for half of them."

It struck Mr Smith's conscience, that had Mr Leslie said he was an absconding swindler, he could hardly have put it much more plainly.

After reflecting again, he took his resolution.

"You have said that you are not curious, and I believe it. If I do make a clean breast of it, as you propose, may I count on your absolute discretion? One word from you will suffice."

Leslie hesitated and shook his head. "I can make no rash promise of the kind. Do you not see, that on your own admission—and you must forgive me the suggestion—I might possibly be pledging myself to be the tacit accomplice in a crime?"

Smith rose as if he meant to cut short the interview; yet he did not go far away. "If you will not pledge yourself, I cannot speak," he said over his shoulder, gruffly and shortly.

Then it was Ralph's turn to think. If he did invite the man's confidence, and become the depositary of some unwelcome secret, society was no worse off than before, nor could the interests of justice suffer. So long as he knew nothing, he could do nothing to help justice. While, on the other hand, if Smith were persuaded to speak at all, he might be prevailed upon to make further confession. Besides, Ralph was urged on by a strange presentiment, oddly inconsistent with the un-inquisitive nature of which he had boasted, but which told him that he might hear something to somebody's advantage. Right or wrong, he did make up his mind.

"If you will tell me anything you wish to tell, Mr 'Smith,'"—and he laid marked emphasis on the pseudo-patronymic,—"I give you my word that it goes no further, unless with your full and free consent."

"Smith" heaved a sigh, as if he were throwing a weight off his breast. "God bless

you, Mr Leslie! I believe you were sent on
board this ship as my better angel. In saving
a life that I have often longed to be rid of,
you may have done me a better service than
I supposed; you may have given me time for
repentance and atonement."

Whereupon he burned his boats, and cut off
all possibility of retreat.

"My name is not Smith, but Mungo
Campbell."

Leslie half jumped from his seat, but in-
continently recollecting himself, sat down
again.

"What! You have heard that name before. Ay—Leslie—Leslie—of course you are
a Scotsman, though you have not a touch of
the accent I have tried indifferently to conceal.
I trust in heaven, sir, that you were not one
of the shareholders of that unhappy bank."

"I held no shares myself," answered Leslie;
then he added with deliberate honesty, "but
dear friends of mine have been ruined."

"The finger of Providence!—the finger of
Providence!" exclaimed the other. "It has
always been tracking me and pointing at me,
and now it has brought me to my knees."

There was a light, almost like that of in-
sanity, in his eyes. It told a terrible tale of
internal struggles, and of prolonged mental
sufferings. Leslie felt himself torn asunder
between the promptings of indignation and
compassion. Then this Cain, who had been
driven from society with the brand of infamy
on his forehead, settled down into the calm
and methodical man of business. The habit
of business seemed to have carried him back
from the Red Sea trip to the counting-house
in Buchanan Street, within rifle-shot of the
Broomielaw. He expounded facts and figures
clearly enough—sensational facts, and most
startling figures. By way of confirmation, he
produced from a breast-pocket a note-book
filled with precise memoranda.

"They advertised a reward of a couple of
thousand pounds for my apprehension," he
said; "and had they offered ten, ay, or twenty
times as much, they would have had a cheap
bargain could they have caught me and com-
pelled me to speak. They knew I was in-
debted to the bank in over a million. They
knew I was far the largest shareholder besides.
But they fancied I had been brought to grief

by mad speculation—that the assets I could show were not worth counting upon. Well, they were wrong. When I told my colleagues and fellow-swindlers, who began latterly to worry me, that I only wanted time to work round, I was speaking the solemn truth. Being living lies themselves, and sharp men of business to boot, it was but natural that they should not believe a word of it. It was true that for the time I had neither cash nor credit, and when the bank stopped further supplies I was brought to a deadlock. The smash we had been expecting had come at last, and there was nothing left but to be gone. All my plans had been laid; all my precautions were taken. While my thoughts were riveted to the stone and lime of our bank premises as fast and firm as any of our fire-proof safes, my body had gone cruising in my steam-yacht from my summer residence on the coast of Argyleshire. I was landed at Belfast. I covered my trail, and took shipping from Queenstown for America, whither I had consigned the bulk of my treasure. The sums I had been borrowing from the shareholders of the bank had been duly trans-

mitted beyond the Atlantic. I was nearly as
cute as the world had given me credit for
being; and my only fault, from the business
point of view, was that of being over-sanguine.
The seed I had sown was to bear fruit many-
fold, but I had counted upon reaping before
the time of the harvest. In fact, owing to
family connections, I had launched out audaciously in American speculations — raising
money upon one to invest it in another.
Worse luck for me, I had only too good information. I had gone shares in promising
mining claims; I had sunk large sums in de-
veloping them. I was an active member in
a syndicate that was financing a trans-con-
tinental line of railway, with vast concessions
of State domains that could only be gradually
realised, and we were at close grips for the
moment with Jay Gould and Vanderbilt. I
was far in with a 'cotton corner' at New
York. Never was there such a combination
of temporary ill-luck; but from the moment
that Providence came down upon me and
drove me forth from my kind — from that
moment the tide began to turn."

"One thing puzzles me," interposed Leslie,

who had been lending a most attentive and
business-like ear, "and that is, how the liquidators, who have a claim on your estate, were
unable to hit upon the trace of those investments. I know something about it, for I have
been looking into the bank's affairs," he added.

"I do not know how you should come to be
so well informed about the bankruptcy affairs,
but being so, it is very natural you should ask
the question. And if, like most Scots, you
are curious in metaphysics, I can submit a remarkable psychological phenomenon for your
study. Sanguine as I was, I knew I was
running a match against luck and time, and
I did my best to take measures accordingly.
All chances weighed, it seemed to me more
prudent to stake on the honesty of an individual I believed I knew, rather than trust
everything to time or circumstances. The
whole of those American transactions were
undertaken in the name of a man who is my
nephew by marriage. He will die either a
millionaire or a beggar — there is no mean
for him. He is perhaps the shrewdest fellow
I ever met; yet, strange to say, he has been
absolutely true to me. How he reconciles

things to his conscience all round, I cannot
tell; for he is in the secret of my eclipse and
false name, and he knows well that I am
badly wanted by the liquidators. He prides
himself on being a 'smart man'; he could
repudiate me and appropriate my possessions
at any moment.   Yet he has always accounted
to me for every dollar : he is trustee at this
moment of vast accumulations, reinvested at
handsome prospective profits ; and, in short,
has hitherto been always on the square with
me, though he may have behaved to the bank
and its creditors like a scoundrel."

Leslie sat thoughtful and speechless.   With
the money that this man could repay, the load
of the bank's liabilities would be so lightened,
that Moray, were he indeed alive, might have
come home again the master of Glenconan—
that Grace might have become his own wife
to-morrow, with easy mind and a comfortable
income.

Too late ! Too late ! This infernal swindler,
and such as he, had been the death of a man
who was worth ten thousand of him, and
wrecked the future which might have been
so bright and prosperous.

Smith, or Mr Mungo Campbell, talked or "maundered" on. He seemed to have forgotten the presence of his father - confessor, and was following out the train of his thoughts. He was unconscious that in talking to the kind-hearted stranger who had been his sicknurse, he was playing within reach of the claws of a tiger; for Leslie for the time had wellnigh lost his self-control, and was struggling with passions that almost maddened him.

"How can we explain those inconsistencies of moral character?" proceeded Mr "Smith," indulging his metaphysical speculations on the brink of the invisible abyss. "And yet it is stranger still to think, looking back, how I could ever have lowered myself to such depths of rascality. Would you know what I suffered in slipping down the hill? God forbid that you should ever learn it by experience. According to the classics, the descent to Avernus is easy; but the Bible says that the ways of transgressors are hard. And the Bible morality, as usual, has the best of it. They tell you I was the vilest of hypocrites when I gave my money to churches and charities. Not a bit of it. I delighted in doing generous actions

for their own sake; and if I confess that I was
in too great haste to grow rich, still I believe
I should have sanctified my fortune to good
works when I had amassed it, and might have
died in the odour of benevolence, like a Pea-
body or a Sir Joseph Mason.   It was a headlong
race against Time, and Time won it by a neck
or so.   That is God's own truth; and so may
God help me, for He only knows how I have
suffered!"

And then, worn out by agitation and weakened by recent illness, the fugitive director
dropped his face in his hands, and broke down
in a storm of sobs and tears.

CHAPTER XXXVI.

PENITENT AND CONFESSOR.

RALPH would have been soft as warm wax to the weeping of a woman, and it was almost worse with him when he saw this man crushed down under the weight of his sins and sorrows. His indignation was hot as ever; his anger was already half disarmed. If the sinner should prove his penitence by making ample atonement, why, he would try to forgive him, as he trusted that God might.

"Do you fancy I have been the happier," said Smith, exciting himself again, "that I have kept my person out of the clutches of the law, and saved my treasure as well?—my treasure!" and in the way in which he uttered the word there was a world of commentary on the text that all we most covet is vanity.

Ralph saw his opportunity and seized it.

" Assuredly not; what can all your money profit you? more than a millionaire, and a hunted fugitive going about with a price on your head and a slight disguise that may slip from you again, as circumstances have stripped it from you now! So little do I fancy it, that I believe no man could do you a greater kindness than by persuading your better judgment that it would be best to go straight back to Scotland."

The instincts of self-preservation are strong, especially when they have been ingrained as the habits of one's life. With the lights of semi-insanity flickering in his eyes, Smith looked at Ralph with a glance of furtive suspicion. "You are thinking already of going back from your word; you mean to betray me into the hands of my enemies."

And he paced the deck with short irregular strides, swinging his arms about, and muttering sullenly to himself. Another man might have been sorely tempted to give him up, and might have justified the breach of promise by specious casuistry. Like Herod, Ralph might have said to himself, " I have given a hasty pledge; but have I any right to hold myself to it, considering the interests that are affected?" But Ralph had no idea of tampering with evil that good might come, and it was his principle that honesty was the best policy in all circumstances.

"A man of honour has only his word, and I don't go back from mine, even when——"

"Even when you are dealing with a scoundrel steeped in dishonour to the lips?"

"I did not say so, nor did I mean it altogether. I see you have suffered intensely, Mr Campbell. Nevertheless, you will forgive my saying that I know you too little to judge how far your penitence may be sincere. But this I do know, that no man, situated as you are, had ever a grander opportunity of retrieving great part of the misery he has helped to cause. May I ask," he added, abruptly, "what scheme of life you have sketched out for yourself,—what are your immediate intentions in wandering like the wandering Jew?"

Smith looked at him in surprise, and broke out bitterly. "Need you ask about my future? Of course it is a blank; and as for my immediate objects, I do not know that they greatly concern you. But forgive me; I am wrong, and I forget my debt to you. As I have told so much, I may tell you more; and after all, what does it all matter? I consulted doctors in Spain : they warned me that I was threatened by consumption,—that one lung was seriously affected already. They said that my best chance was prolonged residence in some tropical climate ; and it struck me I might try Java, where I should be little likely to meet with old acquaintances. People say it is a paradise too; if so, it was my only chance of getting a glimpse at heaven."

There was so much of sadness and of despair in his tone, that for the moment other considerations were swallowed up in Ralph's compassion. It was for Campbell's own sake, not for that of the Morays—if they were alive —that he pled with the fugitive earnestly and eloquently.

"You may yet see another heaven than the Spice Islands, if you will only listen while still there is time. The door of retreat, the way of noble reparation, is still open to you. But should you shut the door now, with your own hand and with your eyes open, the sufferings that have aged you and broken you ere now, will be nothing to those you will endure for the future. I speak it solemnly, and I know what I am saying. The heaven] you are seeking in the Dutch settlements will be the sure foretaste of hell."

Mr Leslie, it will be admitted, had put the case pretty strongly, and he walked away, leaving his words to work. He guessed shrewdly at the other man's nature and feelings. He knew that after all Campbell had gone through, the feeling that he might be at the crisis of his fate would weigh with him more than anything. For long he had resigned himself to hopeless despondency. Ralph had shown him that there were still glimmerings of hope which might brighten into comfort again or be quenched in despair. And he believed that "Smith" would feel all depended on his present decision.

Nor did those shrewd calculations deceive him. After an anxious half-hour, his penitent came up more cheerful than he had seen him before. He spoke humbly and quietly, yet with more of the air of an equal; and the prospect of retracing his steps had taken some of the stoop out of his shoulders.

" I am likely to owe you something more than my life, Mr Leslie. I have come to you for advice, or rather for instructions. I put myself absolutely in your hands."

" Let me understand you," said Ralph, speaking very quickly, and vainly struggling to repress his emotions. " You really mean to act as I shall counsel you ? "

" Can you look in my face, Mr Leslie, and doubt it ? Can you be so blind as not to see that your prescriptions have done me good already. You are a tender sick-nurse, as I know well ; but believe me, you are a better doctor for the mind diseased than for the body. My mind, such as it is, is made up. I go ashore at Penang ; I go back to Glasgow ; and perhaps it is the best pledge of my sincerity, that in so doing I sacrifice my life. The air of a Scotch jail is scarcely likely to be so beneficial for a consumptive as the breath of the cinnamon and nutmeg groves of the South."

What Campbell said was extremely natural ; yet, after all, it was an unpleasant way of putting it. It made Leslie act the executioner, as well as the confessor and the judge, and sentence the victim before him to slow but certain death.

Leslie might have hesitated, but he would not have drawn back. He had no idea at any cost of compromising with what was right, and that Campbell was taking the right course was evident. But had he felt serious embarrassment, Campbell would have come to the rescue.

"And should I die in prison, or in shame and destitution, I shall be more grateful to you for your advice, than for your help in the cabin below here. We understand each other, and no more need be said."

On second thoughts, however, it struck our friend that something more ought to be said. He knew little of Campbell, and had no strong faith in sudden conversions. That Campbell was sincere at the present moment he could not doubt; he said that were a detective to turn up with a pair of handcuffs, the culprit would stretch out his hands with satisfaction. But once ashore on the wharves of Penang, exchanging the close confinement of the ship for the bustle of successful traffic, beyond the reach of Leslie's presence and influence, the good resolutions might vanish like the visions of an ugly dream, and this slippery customer might slip through their fingers. Where so very much was at stake, it might be safer to communicate with the colonial police; and yet, in the circumstances, such a course was not only ungenerous but actually out of the question.

Here again the intelligent "Mr Smith," his faculties sharpened by penitence and gratitude, helped his preserver out of the dilemma. Having repeatedly marked Ralph's eyes reflectively fixed upon him, and as quickly diverted again on being observed, on one of these occasions Smith walked straight up to him.

"Thanks to you, Mr Leslie, I am in so much better spirits, that were it not a piece of impertinence, I might say, 'A penny for your thoughts.' Though, for the matter of that, I can guess them. You have been puzzling yourself as to what is to be done about me when we arrive at Penang."

Ralph blushed and stammered, but could not deny the impeachment.

"Well, I will tell you what you must do. You must trust everything to me: for the best of reasons,—that you cannot help yourself, not to speak of your being fast tied by your promise. Say you deliver me to the officers; and as there are no warrants out against me in the Settlement, I doubt whether you can do it. Say you detain me and have my identity proved, and send me back to Scotland in custody. *Cui bono?* You see, I remember something of the humanities I picked up at Glasgow High School. I should be punished, no doubt; but the bank would get no pecuniary profit thereby. You could not betray the financial confidences I placed in you; and if you could, each dollar of my American investments is in the name of Van Swindel, my wife's nephew. But leave me free to go and give myself up: I swear that I shall start by the first packet; that I shall make a clean breast of all my delinquencies to the liquidators; and that I shall strip myself of my last shilling for their benefit. The only possible hitch—you see, I play all my cards down on the table—the only possible hitch is that Van Swindel should prove recalcitrant. But judging by the past, I may count on that eccentric honesty of his ; and, in any case, nobody can influence him but I.   That is the situation, Mr Leslie.   What do you say ? "

Leslie had grasped the situation while Campbell was defining it.   If he had any mis-givings, it would have been a mistake to show them ; but now he felt few or none.

" I take your word of honour, Mr Campbell; and I leave everything to your honour and conscience.   You are bound over now to hon-esty by such tremendous penalties, that it is far more your affair than mine or that of my friends.   And I am assured that, as we say in Scotland, in spite of all that has come and gone, you will die the honest man that you used to be, and hold your head high hereafter if not here."

CHAPTER XXXVII.

MISS MORAY'S IRISH CHAMPION.

WE are doomed to endure much needless
misery—none the less real that it is so absolutely gratuitous. Leslie had had fair
reason for the apprehensions that had made
his voyage to the South a prolongation of
torments. But landing at Penang, he learned,
to his delight, that the terrible telegram had
been absolutely baseless. The matter for it
had been traced to some Dutchman at Sarambang, eager to do an injury to the Sumatra
Company. If the sender in any degree believed in his news, the wish must have been
father to the thought, for at the time things
at Sanga were tolerably tranquil. The immediate relief was immense ; second thoughts
in the reaction of feeling were less satisfactory.
For the Company's agents at Penang had re-

ceived recent and more reliable news which
told that troubles were brewing in the Settlement.   The Resident was sanguine that they
could be easily repressed ; but he talked of
a trip to Sarambang, that he might seek a
personal interview with the Sultan.

As Leslie could not borrow the wings
of a bird, he had to make arrangements
as to his passage.   Meantime, as we have
the advantage of him, and can transport
ourselves to the scene of his anxieties, we
may follow the fortunes of Moray and his
daughter.

Moray's first letters, as it may be remembered, were full of hope.   He saw no cause
to disbelieve in a great future for the Settlement.   It was no Poyais scheme, no "wild-
cat" speculation, like the Eden of General
Scadder.   But he foresaw considerable trouble
before arriving at the ends towards which he
was determined to push forward resolutely.
For himself, he had braced all his energies to
a work which he confidently counted on ac-
complishing.   In this beginning of a new life
he had regained his former spirits.   The days
that had been dragging by so wearily before

he left England, were wellnigh forgotten with
the slow liquidation of the Bank claims. He
had left means for meeting all probable calls;
and the loss of the fortune he had passed a
lifetime in amassing was already fading from
his memory. He had his daughter with him
—new interests were opening before him, with
higher aims than mere trading profits and personal aggrandisement. When he had tried his
hand at philanthropy among the masses of
Eastern London, though with a full purse and
practically unlimited credit, he had been but
one in a great army of workers—if not a mere
private in the ranks, at most a non-commis-
sioned officer. Now he was a politician, a
statesman, an autocratic administrator, ruling
a little Principality numbering some 80,000
souls. Nor, with the example of the Rajah
of Sarawak before him, need his influence be
limited to the Company's domain. He might
and he would put down piracy; he would
send messages of peace and goodwill among
his weaker, though warlike, neighbours; he
might do much to accelerate the process of
civilisation that had been barely begun in
the Sultanate of Sarambang. With those

prospects of usefulness opening before him, coloured by a noble if an unavowed ambition, perhaps Moray, settling down in his residential seat at Sanga, was happier than ever he had been before.

His first impressions were only confirmed on further acquaintance. Coal and copper mines had already begun to be wrought; and it was certain they must soon yield remunerative returns. Chinese immigrants were already swinging the cradles at the gold-washings with very satisfactory results. But the real wealth of the Settlement was in the climate and the teeming richness of the soil, wherever the jungle and the forest had been cleared from the banks of the river and its tributaries. To say nothing of the spice-groves that scented the air, the natives were busy already in the sugar and the cotton plantations, which stretched in glossy or snowy shrubberies over alluvial soil, fertilised by immemorial accumulations of leaf-mould. And as a consequence of the security his predecessor had already created, little clusters of dwellings had been rising everywhere on piles in shady nooks and angles

along the river, with the rickety landing-
places of planks, from which the cultivators
shipped their produce.

So far, all was satisfactory. The people
were naturally well disposed to a Government
which gave them the unaccustomed blessings
of peace and plenty. They could sow their
seed with easy minds, now that they were
sure of harvests and of markets for the harvests : they could lie down in quiet under
their bamboo roofs, with no fear that the
village might be in a blaze before morning.
So far, then, all was well; nevertheless Mr
Moray soon discovered that this very tran-
quillity held the germs of trouble for him.
He had to master the politics of the Settlement for himself; for though his subordinates
might be honest, they were certainly dull.
Happily he knew nearly enough of the Malay
language to be able to communicate with his
copper-coloured subjects ; at all events, he
knew more than enough to make it impossible for interpreters to play tricks with him.
And speedily he began to find that in what
he had fancied a comfortable seat, there
were thorns thrusting themselves through the

cushions.   On the one hand, the robber-tribes
in the neighbourhood doubly resented the
new prosperity of the Sanga folks.   In the
first place, they were very naturally jealous ;
and in the next place, they were furious at
being restrained from their prescriptive rights
of reiving and pillage.   More than once or
twice they had tried the old familiar game ;
each time the gallant Chamberlain had beaten
them back or baffled them.   The death of
the firm English chief had given them fresh
courage ; and they had been eager to profit
by the interregnum.   While, on the other
hand, there were Europeans and native princes
as well, all ready to utilise their discontent.
The Sultan of Sarambang was still friendly :
he had a heavy stake, as has been said, in
the wellbeing of the Company.   But the
Sultan of Sarambang was a weak oriental,
and oriental manners prevailed at his Court.
He had a baker's dozen of brothers ; and as
he knew very well, any one of the cadets of
his house would have gladly poisoned or
assassinated him.   He had not the nerve for
a cleansing of the palace, or a domestic *coup
d'état,* which would have effectually quenched

the malevolence in a "blood-bath." Astute foreign traders, presumed to be in the Dutch interest, were intriguing with the malcontent faction and subsidising it. The malcontents were in intimate relations with the tribes of discomfited pirates, already weighing the chances of a successful descent upon Sanga; and these tribes in their turn were believed to be in communication with the scattered inhabitants of the forests of Sanga, who had gained nothing as yet by the English annexation, but who were restrained from their favourite pursuits of robbery, fire-raising, and head-hunting.

That was the situation as Moray saw it in a month, and it may be added that he was not far from the truth.

He thought matters over deliberately, and promptly made up his mind. Like the stoker of the Mississippi steamer in the wild Western ballad, he saw that "his duty was a dead-sure thing," and thenceforward nothing could turn him from his purpose. Nevertheless, already he painfully realised that the sweets of his new post were to be mingled with bitters. He had to break what she would regard as

bitterly bad news to his daughter, and steel
himself against her prayers and her tears.
She had come with him to this barbarous
country at the back of the world, on the tacit
understanding that they were not to be separated.   But now his duty tore them apart :
there was no help for it.   When he told her
that he must make an expedition immediately
to Sarambang, and that he must go alone and
leave her behind ;—to the girl, who was already beginning to give herself over to the
sensuous influences of the balmy air, the soft
beauties of nature, and the tropical *bien-être*,
it was like a flash of lightning out of a cloudless sky.   She would have cared little could
she have accompanied him ; but on that point
he was adamant, and she could not gainsay
his arguments.

"Do not pain me needlessly, Grace, by saying more.   God knows how gladly I would
take you with me !   Had the Company's
steamer been here, I might possibly have done
so.   As it is, it is utterly out of the question.
There is no accommodation for an English
lady in these native boats—and from a native
boat you must land at Sarambang ; and I

would never take my daughter to a barbarous Court."

Put to her in that way, Grace could say no more ; and by this time she knew her father too well to insist. But he was bound, besides, to say something of the reasons for his going ; and soften them down as he might, they were far from reassuring. The very fact that he left her alone, argued his apprehension of some urgent danger. Not that Grace thought very much of herself,—and indeed she was too in- nocent to apprehend the worst. On the con- trary, trying to forget herself and her fears, she set herself to cheer her father.

" Don't make yourself needlessly uneasy about me, papa. I daresay I shall get on very well in your absence. I *would* come out with you, you know, and I am very glad that I came."

But though both Grace and her father wore brave faces, it was all they could do to bear up before the separation. No one of his war- like ancestors had given proof of greater cour- age than Glenconan, when, with a set face that was pale as resolute, he stepped into the great proa that was to carry him to Sarambang.

As for Grace, she had bidden him farewell before breaking down; she had stood waving her hand and her handkerchief as long as the little fleet was in sight—for his own boat was escorted by sundry others, all of them armed to the teeth; and then, in a storm of sobs and tears, she had hurried up to the roof of the Residency. Had she had any thoughts but for a single man, she might have taken comfort from the looks of the native guards, who seemed to understand her desolation and sympathise with it. Afterwards, indeed, she recalled their demeanour to some purpose. From the roof, she followed the fleet with tearful eyes, as it was propelled by the sturdy strokes of the sweeps, round the reaches of the winding river. She seemed to see a happy omen, as it slid, comparatively smoothly, over the seething bar; and still she watched it as, standing out to sea, it steered its course for the dim western headland. The taper masts and yards were covered with light clouds of billowy matting; the sails filled slowly to a favouring breeze; and at last it melted away in the distance, like .a flight of butterflies flickering in the sunset.

She went to bed to weep, and toss, and wear the night away with broken prayers. Never had she dreamed of feeling so utterly desolate, so absolutely unprotected. "Oh, if Ralph were only here!" she moaned to herself again and again; and little did she fancy that very day Ralph had been chafing on the wharves of Penang and cursing the channel that separated them. She saw the night through with those broken prayers, and she rose from the bed next morning a different girl. Not that her very natural apprehensions were calmed. On the contrary, she realised more clearly than before the dangers that might threaten her, and very likely she exaggerated them. But she had all the pluck of the soldiers of her race, whose spirits had risen naturally in critical circumstances. She wished from the very bottom of her heart that she were a man,—though that, unfortunately, was past praying for. Being a woman, however, she might do what no man could do so well, and use her helplessness as a shield against possible dangers. As she had said in the letter to her friend Julia, she believed in the chivalry of the Malays: well, she would put it to the proof, and do her utmost to assure their loyalty. Then, if troubles should break out when her father was away, she might animate the garrison in the defence of the Settlement.

Though she had set herself diligently to the study of the Malay grammar, as yet she had got no further than its A B C. But she was one of those women whose looks and smiles say much; and she had, moreover, a feminine interpreter in whom she could trust. Moray, after mature reflection, had decided on not hampering his daughter with an English maid. But they had picked up a Chinese polyglot at Penang, who spoke broken English fairly well, and was much more fluent in the Malay tongue. Already the girl had become fondly attached to her young mistress. And now Grace and her almond-eyed *suivante*, who followed her like a shadow, were to be seen playing the parts of Eveline Berenger and Rose Flammock before the defence of the Garde Doloureuse. Indeed there was a sinister resemblance in the circumstances which more than once suggested itself to Grace. The part, be it remembered, seemed to come naturally enough to Miss Moray. The daughter of the governor had always appeared to the Malay soldiers as a bright-humoured being from another world. And now, what with her winning smiles and kindly words—what with largesses of food and fruits and liquor,—there was hardly a man of them who might not have been easily intoxicated into running *amok* for the sake of her beautiful eyes. She had done well in losing no time in taking her precautions and using the only weapons she could handle. There were spies in the Settlement in the pay of the Company's enemies; and the news of the Resident's departure, with good part of his fighting force, spread like wildfire among the many who were nearly interested in it.

The late Colonel Chamberlain had been a strong man; but so much could not be said for his secretary and chief subordinate. Mr Briggs, no doubt, was an excellent man of business, and would have made a capital confidential clerk in the City. He was honest as the day, and thoroughly at home in the mysteries of book-keeping and bills of lading. He had drifted from Alexandria southwards to Singapore, and so on to Sumatra; but he was as much abroad in those islands of the

South as a Malay might be on the roof of a metropolitan omnibus. Grace lost patience altogether with the smug and kindly little gentleman, who was always overpoweringly civil, and who would have been paternal had she permitted it. He lived in each day as if there need be no to-morrow. He never seemed to see an inch beyond his small snub nose; and he did his work thoroughly, conscientiously, and well, like an entomologist peering after beetles, who looked at life through the lens of a microscope. He was left as acting Resident, as managing director—all the rest of it. After all, he was not only the senior Englishman, but the best educated man in the Settlement; and Moray, who hoped that everything was safe till his return, could hardly help himself. With much searching of heart, he had confided his unprotected daughter to the special care of Mr Briggs; and the worthy little clerk had undertaken the charge as he would have undertaken any other duty in the routine of his engagements.

For a week or so after her father's departure, all had gone well, and nothing had occurred to increase her anxieties. Shaking herself gradu-

ally free of her fears, as she began to hope for
his speedy return, she was sauntering on the
little lawn between the Residency and the
river late one evening, and in more buoyant
spirits than usual. The serene beauty of the
tropical night — the stars that had already
begun to flash and sparkle, though the sun had
scarcely gone down in a blaze of crimson—the
silent sweep of the great bats through the
scented air—the droning hum of the broad-
winged beetles,—all contributed to soothe her.
Where everything was so peaceful in the star-
spangled twilight, it seemed impossible that
there could be trouble impending. Yet she
might have remembered that nature, like man,
may wear a mask, and that in the dusky soli-
tudes of those silent woods were venomous
serpents and prowling jaguars.

A rustling in the bushes near may have reminded her of the fact. She started with a
half-suppressed shriek; for though a brave
girl, she was but a woman after all, and besides,
there might be very real danger. She was
but partially reassured, when a man, and a
white man, stepped out of the shrubs. She
knew him, as she knew by sight the few Euro-

peans in Sanga; and this "Sergeant" Rafferty,
as he was styled, was one of the most conspicuous of them. She had spoken more than
once to the man, and made sundry inquiries
about him, for he had rather interested her.
There had been a good deal of romance in his
career; and as he said himself, the divil a bit
of use was there in his trying to keep his
sacrets, for they would always come out when
the drink went in. The drink had indeed
been the bane of Mr Rafferty, who might
otherwise have been a creditable member of
the little community. As he further said, it
was the drink that had tumbled him down-
stairs from a dacent position; he had always
holes in his pockets, so that the halfpence
would be for iver rowling out; it was the
drink that had brought him down to this
Sumathra, which he took to be pretty near at
the bottom of the world; and whether he was
to lave his bones there or fall any farther, divil
a one of him either knew or greatly cared. In
fact, neither knowing nor caring summed up
his character; but he had the invaluable
quality under present circumstances of constitutional intrepidity or recklessness.

The Sergeant stepped forward with a military salute. It was noteworthy that the man, usually so ready to talk, waited respectfully for the lonely young lady to address him; for in spite of his foibles and vices, Rafferty was much of a gentleman. And knowing what he came to say, he behaved far more respectfully than if she had been under the escort of her father, the Resident, who had at Sanga almost the power of pit and gallows that had once been possessed by his forefathers in Glenconan.

As for Grace, she had no fear of him, but she felt a foreboding that he was the bearer of evil tidings. She longed to know, yet dreaded to ask; and seeing what was passing in her mind, Rafferty no longer hesitated.

"I should beg you to pardon me, me lady, for staling on you unawares; but sure this is no time for standing on ceremony. I was bint upon spaking without them Malays knowing anything of it; and so I have been kaping a look-out upon the grass here from a bit of a boat on the wather."

"What is it? Do speak, Mr Rafferty!"

"And sure, miss, what else would it be that

I came for? But don't you be botherin' and making yourself unaisy—it may be little after all. I know nothing of that jabber of theirs, bad luck to it! and it will be time enough to cry out when we're hurt."

It was a very Irish piece of comfort, considering that the man had clearly come to warn her of dangers in the hope that they might be prevented. It appeared that the acute Mr Rafferty had seen reason to suspect that something was being plotted somewhere among the natives. The Malays of the Settlement were in a state of excitement which they took little pains to conceal. Scouts had been sent up the river in the long, snake-like light craft; messengers had been coming and going through the jungles. He opined that an attack was threatened, and he greatly doubted whether "thim niggers were to be trusted," who formed the staple of the garrison.

Grace, after questioning the man, shared his alarms and his doubts as well. The Malays had seemed to be friendly towards herself; but nevertheless they might be anxious to be rid of their European masters, and have an

understanding with warriors of their own
blood and colour who might be threatening
Sanga from without. With the Resident and
half his fighting force away they could hardly
have a better opportunity. The natural person she would have consulted in such an
emergency was Mr Briggs, and thinking half
aloud, the name escaped her lips.

"Is it Briggs then?" queried Mr Rafferty,
in tones of infinite contempt. In his disgust
he spat upon the ground, and forthwith became covered with confusion.

"I ask your pardon, miss, from the very
bottom of my heart; but if I had thought
Briggs had anything bigger than the sowl of a
newly hatched chicken, I would never have
come to you."

Grace could not help smiling, her anxiety
notwithstanding. If she did not say so, she
was much of Mr Rafferty's opinion,—though, as
will be seen, they did the little man injustice.
She rapidly reviewed the situation in her
mind. If an attack on the place were really
intended, she felt that the sole chance of
safety was in the loyalty of the native settlers.
After all, they had reason to be satisfied with

a Government which promised them peace as
well as wealth.

Rafferty was disposed respectfully to differ.

"The Lord, He knows well that they're
fond enough of money, come by it how they
may. But as for *pace*, they prefer fighting to
it any day; and why wouldn't they?" he
added, with judicial candour. "I come from
Tipperary myself, and I like them none the
worse for that."

Indeed, Sergeant Rafferty was the sort of
man who would have smoked his pipe on a
powder-barrel, and found the situation lend
additional flavour to his tobacco. His sole idea
in coming to Grace seemed to have been to
volunteer to defend her and the Residency
with his single arm. But he was open to
conviction, and she succeeded in persuading
him that it was improbable that any single
man could protect four sides of an extensive
square against assailants practically innumerable.

"I might be murdered, sure enough—not
that it signifies; but what would become of
you? Sowl of the blessed St Pathrick, what
will we do thin, at all, at all?"

" Will you do what I ask you, Rafferty ? "

" What else did I come for ? You may count on Jack Rafferty, body and spirit, till your father comes back, and beyond that."

" God grant he might come back ! Well, Rafferty, you know where to find Matusin ? "

Matusin was one of the former chiefs of Sanga, and now occupied a semi-official position as head man of the native community. In short, it was through Matusin that the Resident directed great part of the domestic politics.

" I can find the blayguard fast enough. Unless the divil has stirred him up to do mischief, he'll be sitting smoking and drinking all the night with the rest of them. Bedad, but it's they nigger chiefs that have the fine time of it ! "

" Well, will you go straight to Matusin from me ? show him this ring of mine, and ask him to come to the Residency here, and to come at once. I don't think there is any danger for you; and if there were, I am sure it would not hinder you from doing my errand."

Mr Rafferty snorted contemptuously at the word danger, and did not even deign a reply to that part of the speech. "But how if he would refuse to come?"

"I don't think that he will. Whatever his intentions, he is strong enough to act as he pleases. Go on my errand at any rate. We must leave the rest to God."

Rafferty took the ring and made a dart at the bushes, through which lay the nearest way to his boat. Then, struck by a thought, he hurried back. "But if he should refuse to come, and should keep howld of me, you will never believe that I desaved you, miss?"

"No, no, Rafferty. I trust you as I would trust my father, were he here."

"Then by this and that"—and Rafferty dropped on one knee with instinctive chivalry,—"by this and that, and till I have seen you safe through this blessed business, not a drop of drink shall pass my lips, were they as cracked as the 'craythur,' as they call it, on the mountain behind."

And Grace felt very grateful to the man for the pledge of devotion, though she could scarcely appreciate all the sublimity of his sacrifice.

CHAPTER XXXVIII.

A MODERN EVELINE BERENGER.

WHEN she had despatched her messenger, Grace felt anxious enough. More than she dared to think of depended on the coming interview; for that it would be granted, she did not doubt. But in the meantime there was something to be done in the way of preparation. The sending the ring had been a stroke of diplomacy: it was the symbol of an authority she did not possess. Her real strength, as she felt, was in her weakness, in her youth and her unprotected situation. She hoped to appeal to the Malay's chivalry as well as to his self-interest. So she made hasty arrangements to set her house in order; she had the state room disposed with an eye to effect; and last, though by no means least, she made certain alterations in her toilet.

Then she warned her faithful maid to be ready
to act as interpreter, though Matusin had some
slight knowledge of English, and so, to a certain extent, she could communicate with him
directly.

Her suspense did not last long, and it was
just as well; for when she had nothing further
to busy herself over, she began to feel painfully nervous. The feeling passed away, when,
looking out from the verandah, she heard the
plash of the oars in the stream, and saw the
flashing of scores of torches. Matusin was
coming to make his visit in state. Was he
coming as a master to dictate his terms, or as
the loyal burgomaster of Sanga, to pay his
duty to the Resident's daughter?

She glided back from the verandah into the
room and waited; she could hear the wild
beating of her heart. It seemed a good omen
that her visitors were landing in dignified
silence; and now that suspense was drawing
to an end, and the critical moment approached,
her courage rose to face the occasion.

The hangings of matting were drawn aside,
and Matusin stood in the doorway. The
Malay had a certain air of dignity: he was

somewhat past middle age, rather a bulky
man, and his dignity was set off by his dress
and draperies.   He wore the usual costume of
a chief of his station and wealth—a dark-green
velvet jacket, the collar stiffened with heavy
tracery of gold-thread; loose trousers of dark
cloth, likewise edged with gold, and a flowing
sarong of the soft dark plaid that is woven by
the women in their native looms.   A couple
of *krises* with richly chased handles were
thrust through his girdle.   And immediately
behind this stately apparition—and a cheering sight it was to Miss Moray, for it seemed
to imply a friendly understanding with the
natives — was Mr Rafferty, evidently on his
best behaviour, but nevertheless winking in-
timations of encouragement.

Had she known all that was passing in her
visitor's mind, she might have been less satisfied.   Indeed, Matusin was in two minds
rather than one, and her message had reached
him in the nick of time, when a decision was
trembling in the balance.   The Malay was
chivalrous in his way, and courageous to boot,
but at the same time, like most orientals, an
accomplished hypocrite.   He was full of grace-

ful observance, and almost obsequious deference, to the Resident's daughter; while he was
thinking whether it were not probable that,
himself aiding and abetting, she might not be
a slave and a captive within four-and-twenty
hours.   Had she shown signs of feebleness,
her fate might have been sealed.   But Grace's
natural courage had been animated by the
belief that she could count upon Matusin's
support and friendship; and in the reaction of
her spirits, she spoke with a confidence that
did not fail to produce its effect.   Matusin
was a well-informed and intelligent man, and
he knew something of the tenacity with which
Europeans kept their hold on any place they
had once touched with the tips of their fingers.
He knew the Sultan of Sarambang favoured
the white strangers; and for himself, he would
gladly perpetuate a state of things which had
greatly increased his wealth, if it had dimin-
ished his personal consequence.   Grace's confidence began to gain upon him : he fancied
the girl could never have shown such spirit
had she not reason to know that her father
was at hand with powerful succour.   Matusin
had a rather formidable fighting force at his

disposal, in a stockaded town; moreover, he had old allies and acquaintances among the armed bands that were threatening it, and he pretty nearly came to the conclusion that it would be well to stand by the English.

So, from being ceremoniously reverential he became blandly confidential, and told the stately young lady nearly all he knew. Certain of the forest-tribes in the Sanga territories, stirred up by agents and strengthened by bands from beyond the frontiers, had determined to make themselves masters of the Settlement either by arrangement with the inhabitants or by assault. They said, too,—and Matusin was inclined to believe it,—that a piratical fleet from the territories to the southward was mustering for their support. So much Grace gathered, partly from the chief's broken English, partly from the interpretation of her handmaiden. Then in turn she began to speak with an energy and cogency of argument which surprised herself. In seeming to trust implicitly to Matusin's loyalty, she appealed strongly to his self-interest. When she remarked that, should their enemies get possession of the place, he would infallibly be pillaged sooner

or later, it was very evident that he understood her, and dare not say Nay. Then she
spoke of the speedy arrival of her father; of
his courage and generosity; of the deep revenge he should take on any one who should
play him false or injure his daughter; on the
rewards he would freely lavish on the faithful
friends who should defend her. I do not say
that her charms and her commanding manner
weighed with the Malay chief as much as her
arguments; but undoubtedly they had no
small influence on him. By the prophet and
the holy stone, by all the most solemn pledges
binding on his countrymen, he vowed that
Sanga should be defended till the return of
the great white Sultan, unless—and the gesture that ended the sentence implied—unless
the assailants should pass over his corpse.
Grace thanked her native champion, and dismissed him with the graceful affability of a
princess born in the purple.

Rightly or wrongly she believed in him,
and so far she felt greatly relieved. At the
same time, it was no light matter to be left
there in her loneliness, looking forward to
the probability of a bloody assault, and a

succession of skirmishes or battles to be fought
out by savages. And even should the assailants be repulsed from the Settlement, if
there were truth in the rumours of the gathering of that piratical fleet, it might come from
the southward to the aid of their· enemies
before her father could appear from the north.
And yet, by the way, if Moray knew what
was happening at Sanga, ·he might surely
obtain succour from the Sultan.

Shaking off her terrors as best she could,
and trusting herself to the God of the helpless, she determined to do all that could be
done. There was no reason to despair, but
there was urgent necessity for action. Within
an hour one of the swiftest proas belonging
to the Company, and manned by men whom
Rafferty believed he could answer for, had
been despatched to Sarambang with letters
for her father.

She went through the form of going to
bed, but she was up again before the larks,
or the birds that answer to our larks in
these southern latitudes. Under the guard
of Mr Rafferty, though she made him leave
his arms behind, for she was resolved to show

absolute confidence in the natives — "Divil
a wan of me would thrust them," soliloquised
her escort, as he concealed a knife and a
couple of revolvers in his ample shirt-bosom
—she went the round of the straggling town.
She had every reason to be satisfied with
what she saw. Matusin was clearly preparing to defend himself in earnest. He had set
gangs of his people to work on the stockades,
strengthening the stakes and building up the
breaches. The women were cutting down
the rank weeds and clearing soil from the
bottoms of the ditches; the men were stack-
ing piles of ammunition near some half-dozen
of light field-pieces and howitzers that grinned
here and there out of embrasures in low earth-
works. But what showed more than anything else that the Malay chief meant fighting, was the measures that were being taken
immediately above the town. Where the
Sánga river contracted into a narrow channel,
running between steep banks overhung with
shrubbery, a great tree was being felled on
either side. One of them came down with
a crash as she reached the spot, sending
the showers of spray into her face, and form-

ing an abattis of foliage impracticable to any
boat, beneath the huge trunk that spanned the
stream by way of a rough sylvan flying-bridge.

"Bedad, but we should be safe in that
quarter anyhow!" exclaimed Rafferty; "and
thim barbarous niggers must have the hides
of their alligators if they find their way through
the bushes there, even in open order, without
laving both skin and flesh behind."

For eight-and-forty hours there was no
great change in the situation. Incidents and
excitement there were in abundance, with perpetual "alarms," as they say in the stage
directions of the old plays. That the beleaguering savages were abroad with fire and sword
there could be no manner of doubt. Boats
came shooting down the river, bearing home-
less fugitives wailing piteously for the relatives who had been slaughtered under their
eyes or carried away into a captivity worse
than death. Confirmatory evidence came in
the shape of the mutilated corpses that floated
down the stream, to be brought up by the
branches of the improvised abattis. The fugitives told tales of sacked villages, of flames
spreading far and wide through their crops

and their orchards, where everything was dry
as tinder after a protracted drought. Grace
shuddered as she listened to the horrible
stories : with a woman's sympathy she did all
a woman could do who knew nothing of the
speech of the fugitives, to relieve the destitute
and to console the bereaved. But all the same,
in the practical turn of the heroism which felt
bound to preserve the Settlement for which
her father was responsible, she neglected no
opportunity of impressing the moral of those
events on Matusin. If the enemy remorse-
lessly plundered the miserable peasants who
had neither dared nor tried to defend themselves, how would they deal with a man who
was notoriously rich, and who had identified
himself with the hated occupation of the English? But Matusin, having once taken the
leap, was like the willing horse who needs no
spurring. He knew now that in the event
of the place being taken he had little mercy
to expect,—that he must sink or swim with
the handful of Europeans.

During the daytime things were comparatively tranquil ; but through two successive
nights the dusky starlight was made terrible

by sights and sounds that kept the garrison
on the alert.   Scarcely had the sun gone down
before there was a descent of flotillas of boats
on the upper reaches of the river.   Thanks
to the felled trees that blocked the water-
way, these flotillas were safe from any counter-
attack.   And each of the boats was illuminated by a fire in a brazier; on board of each
was one or more war-gongs : and each night
these infernal illuminations and diabolical con-
certs were provided for the excitement of the
inhabitants of Sanga.

It was strange to see how differently the
handful of Europeans was affected by the unfamiliar dangers that threatened them.   There
were men who might have been brave enough
in an ordinary way, when blended in the rank
and file of a regiment, who became absolutely
helpless in their fear of this barbarian onslaught,
as certain savages of those forests are paralysed
in presence of the python.   The whites had
been drawn back into the Residency, and em-
ployed in strengthening its defences by way
of a citadel; though some of them who knew
something of serving guns were told off to
the field-pieces on the first line of defence.

So that Grace had every opportunity of study-
ing their characters, which she did, very much
to her own surprise, as if it were a problem
with little personal interest for her. In fact,
what with excitement and want of sleep, she
was living in a factitious state of exaltation,
though her brain was clearer and her resolutions were more prompt than she had ever
known them before.

She remarked that the volatile and hare-
brained Mr Rafferty, when the immediate
work of provisionally fortifying the Residency
was done, had become almost phlegmatic.
Though always ready to spring to attention
when she came near, though he would follow
her with the fidelity and jealousy of a favourite dog, yet at other times he would smoke
cheroots with his hands in his pockets; he
was lulled into tranquil slumbers by the dis-
cord of the rebel gongs; and as he might
have said himself, he seemed to be "blue-
moulded for want of the bating he was very
likely to get."

But if Rafferty's demeanour surprised her,
she was still more astonished by the behaviour
of Mr Briggs. The little man had as little

amour propre; and when she told him, with some hesitation, of the important arrangements she had made without consulting him, he had not stood for a moment on his dignity as nominally the deputy-governor. So, as the best of women might do, she of course took advantage of his weakness, and simply gave him something like peremptory orders to come under the shelter of the Residency.

"As it is to be a sort of inner citadel of the defence, Mr Briggs, you will be safe there, if you are safe anywhere."

Had a crushed worm turned under her slipper, and, speaking like the ass of the prophet, expostulated against being trodden upon, she could scarcely have been more taken aback than when Briggs showed a will of his own, and determination.

"You have taken over the charge of the Settlement and the Residency, Miss Moray, and I do not blame you. You may be more competent than I am, and I daresay you may have as good a right. I see that you can do much with Matusin and his Malays, and therefore I said nothing. But your father at least left the cash-box and the state papers in my charge, and no fear of consequences shall induce me to be parted from them."

"But why should you, Mr Briggs?" exclaimed Grace, greatly touched. "I ought to have considered your feelings more, perhaps, but I had no idea you felt so strongly. You can bring the money and the papers with you, you know : they will be safer in the Residency than anywhere else."

"Pardon me again, madam," said the little gentleman, by no means soothed, and with more formality than before. "Even if I could find trustworthy bearers to transport what money there is—and much of it is in silver, and consequently bulky—the papers are in the fire-proof safe that Colonel Chamberlain ordered out from Cannon Street. It is built into the brickwork, and it is out of the question moving it."

"Of course ; but my father has left you the key, I suppose. Bring the papers to the house here, and we can bury the money in the garden."

"As it is probable that there will be a conflagration in the Settlement to-day or to-morrow, the place of those important papers is in Chubb's patent fire-proof safe. Should they perish there, I cannot help it; and I think the Malays will have trouble in picking the lock. Should they be lost or destroyed elsewhere, I should be justly held responsible. Ah, miss," went on the little man, as he warmed up, "you thought I was a coward, not worthy of a word or a thought; and so perhaps I may be. You might have thought still worse of me had you known all the misery I have gone through from the sound of those abominable gongs. But I do know my duty; I know how I earn my salary, and my place is by the safe and the cash-box. The Malays may tear me limb from limb, or burn me at a slow fire, as they have done to better men on smaller provocation; at least I shall die at my post, and you shall see that a clerk may be a martyr."

"And a hero, Mr Briggs," returned Grace, with a smile that went to his heart, through the tears that wellnigh blinded her. "One thing is, that should you die as you say, none of the rest of us will be left to mourn for you. But if we live, as I believe we shall, and see brighter days, be sure that I for one shall do justice to your heroism."

In such a state of things suspense could not be greatly prolonged; and it was just as well, since human nerve-power has its limits. That afternoon Grace's spirits involuntarily fell: excitement was sinking down into intense depression. So it was more or less with the rest of the Europeans; for the heavens and the very air seemed pregnant with ominous portents. The murky atmosphere had been thickening all the day, and by the evening was overcharged with electricity. Black banks of clouds, gathering over the sea, had been shifting inland, till the bright sky was hidden behind a lowering canopy, which seemed to rest on the tops of the tallest cocoa-nut palms. Sea-birds had been floating landward with the clouds, either flying low in the unnatural silence, or occasionally uttering a plaintive cry. The air was hot—hot—and as yet there was no sign of rain; and those who watched the signs of the weather would have welcomed the threatened deluge, were it only to draw away impending conflagration, for it seemed as if one spark might set everything in a blaze.

The fire came before the water. Grace,

wandering between her rooms and the verandah like a restless spirit, dropped involuntarily into the nearest chair, and covered her
eyes with her hands; while her maid, though
used to tropical thunderstorms, was sending
out shriek on shriek. The strange stillness
had been suddenly broken by a roar over
the roof of the Residency, as if several tons of
dynamite had exploded right over the thatch.
The deafening peal, if peal it could be called,
which sounded like the simultaneous discharge
of the world's parks of artillery, was accompanied, rather than preceded, by a blinding
blaze of light, that flashed home to her brain
through shut eyes and crossed fingers. Then
after that appalling salvo, the cannon of the
heavens began to play, in dropping discharges
at irregular intervals; and once, confused as
she was, she could distinctly distinguish the
crashing and shivering of timber on the lawn
under the windows. How long she sat, with
swimming brain, in the prostration of terror
and soul-mastering awe, she never knew. She
was roused from her stupor by Rafferty bursting into the room, without going through the
ceremony of knocking—though indeed, had

he opened the door with a grenade, it could
hardly have made much difference. Nor was
the appearance of that faithful follower calcu-
lated to reassure her. The devil-may-care
Irishman was pale as death, and muttering
invocations to the Blessed Virgin. Still the
presence of the man helped to bring her to
herself. She found strength to stand upon
her trembling limbs; and reaching out a hand
to seize his arm, she staggered back to the
verandah. After all, as she tried to tell herself, she had never been afraid of English
thunder; and were it not for nerves that had
been painfully overstrained, she would not
have been frightened now. At another time
indeed, and had her father's arm been around
her, she might have admired the tremendous
magnificence of the spectacle. One moment
there was a black darkness that might be
felt; the next, the veil would be rent as by
the mighty hand of the Invisible and Omni-
potent, and the lacery of each leaf and twig
stood out in a lurid illumination that might
have come from Hades, or from anywhere
between heaven and hell. And as she stood
and gazed and trembled, after a wilder peal

a brilliant meteor, shooting swiftly across the
night, pitched under a mighty areca-tree on
the lawn, and seemed to *ricochet* in rippling
electricity over the river.

"May God be good to us all!" ejaculated
Rafferty, through chattering teeth; and then,
remembering that he was the sworn champion
of the lady who still leaned on him, he went
on—"Not that wan of. me cares much; and
after all is said and done, miss, thim divils
outside will never stir in this weather. May
the saints forgive me for spaking of divils!"

As if in answer to him, a preternaturally
long lull was broken by sounds that seemed
insignificant to those that had gone before;
and yet they were ominous of a more terrible
danger. There came a clashing of the gongs
and a shouting of war-cries from the Malay
posts; and as the clamour would occasionally
sink and fall, Grace fancied she could hear
them answered from the distance by something like faint echoes.

Mr Rafferty had no doubt on the matter.
The wild Irishman had sharp ears; and now
that he realised a danger that was material
and tangible, Richard was himself again.

"I spoke too soon, miss—and just like me! I might have known the divils would be at home, and abroad too, in their own particular ilement of fire and sulphur. Luckily, there's little to choose between our friends and them, and our niggers have got the stockades and the guns before them. Anyhow, it is high time I was laving you."

"But your place is in the house here," Rafferty.

"And so I will be in my place when the attack comes this way; but in the manetime, the fun is up the river, and Mister Mathieson may have his hands full. I'll just lave Jackson in charge, and be back again, if need be, in a pig's whisper."

"You are right; we must show ourselves to the Malays at first. Nay, it is no use your objecting; I am going with you to Matusin. I can come back with you."

Rafferty lost no time in protesting, as a more prudent and responsible individual might have done. He felt, besides, that protests would be idle—and there he was right. Miss Moray was submissive to her father, but would have her way with everybody else. In five minutes they had given certain directions; they had crossed the lawn, and Rafferty had handed the lady into a boat. Pulling steadily against the stream, in lightning that lighted the clear water to its depths, in five minutes more they surprised the Malay chief. His admiration of the heroic English girl was extreme, though he had little leisure to express it. As his eyes lighted up to give her a welcome, Grace felt that her visit had been well-timed. It was certain that the Malays would fight more stanchly for having seen that she exposed herself to danger with indifference. But all the more easily she yielded to the joint expostulations of the chief and Rafferty, and withdrew to the shelter of a hut on a little rising ground in the rear of the attack and defence. Thence, from a "front place" beneath a cluster of feathering palms, she could see all that was to be seen.

Not that what was to be seen was much. There was "more cry than wool," more noise made than damage done. The opposing forces, separated by the fallen trees and the impervious jungle, exchanged provocations and missiles, without the possibility of coming to close quarters.

" Ach, sure, thin," remarked Rafferty, who had come back to her in disgust, "for all the fine show they made, coming out in the thunder, they are but braggarts after all.   It was not worth turning out, with the chance of getting wet to the skin, to see nothing more than a solitary nigger with a spent musket-ball in his instep.   They can be no great captains that are against us; and I'd back Mister Mathieson against them any day."

As to putting his money on Mr Matusin, Rafferty might have been right; but he had underrated the strategy of the beleaguering forces.   Though the noisy attack was kept up, he escorted Miss Moray back to the Residency. The storm had pretty well passed over, and the danger seemed to have passed with it. Breathing a heartfelt prayer of gratitude for a double escape from danger, she sank back into the chair she had quitted some hours before, and ordered her servants to provide Rafferty with refreshments.

Prayers can never be misplaced, but the orm of this one was rather premature.   I do

not think 1 have dwelt before on the topo-
graphy of the town of Sanga; but it may be
mentioned now that the Residency had been
built rather with an eye to commercial advantages and beauty of situation than to strateg-
ical considerations. Sanga, in fact, was meant
for a trading town, not for a fortress; and the
Residency stood on a reach of the river, in a
receding back angle of the stockaded works.
It was surrounded by lawns, by gardens and
orchards; and beyond, the jungle came nearly
up to the stockades. It is true that the jungles were so thick that they might have been
regarded as an additional protection, even
against such assailants as the Malays of those
forests.

Grace, then, was lying back in her chair,
and Rafferty, after having apologised for the
familiarity with an indifferent assumption of
bashfulness, had begun vigorously to handle
a knife and fork, when the young lady, doomed
to an ascending gamut of sensations, sprang a
second time out of her seat. This time it was
no noise from the heavens that she heard; the
sound seemed rather and unmistakably to
come from the opposite quarter.

The beleaguering chiefs having assured themselves of the difficulty of forcing the abattis,
had ordered a feigned attack on it. The real
onslaught was to be directed against two other
places, and one of these was the Residency.
But if there are miscalculations in the com-
binations of scientific warfare, barbarians are
still more likely to miss connections. The
force that was to "swarm up" to the Residency was made up of men from three mutu-
ally jealous tribes. One of the bands had gone
astray; a second had been brought to a deadlock in a sylvan *impasse;* and the third, in
their pride and triumph at having arrived,
had forgotten all their savage sagacity and
prudence. They had reached the stockade,
and were scrambling over it unobserved, when
the foremost of them began to whoop and to
halloo. The untimely demonstration gave the
alarm to a native guard who had been bivouacked between the Residency and its outworks.
The friendly Malays, seizing their weapons,
fell hastily back upon the house, which had
been provisionally fortified against the probabilities of disaster. So that the natives,
backed up by the European reserves, were

ready to make a good fight of it under cover.

Yet the assailants were so audacious, and so reckless of their lives, that they might have made their way into the house notwithstanding a stubborn defence. They crept forward, through bushes which ought to have been cut down, to the very foot of the balconies. More than one of them actually tried to climb the pillars which supported the verandahs of the first floor. Grace, peeping downwards through the jalousies, looked down into fiercely gleaming eyes and rolling white eyeballs. Then the eye would be eclipsed, as a death-shot or a stab from above struck the owner; and he would disappear with a dull thud in the dimness, rolling backwards in the agonies of death. But the attack was not effectually repulsed till Rafferty set himself seriously to direct the fire of a rocket-tube. Then the natives were seized with such superstitious terrors as they had never experienced through the worst of the storm. They shrank back from these missiles, which seemed to follow them and search them out like sentient beings, through the very labyrinths and intricacies of the jungle. There

was a panic and a "save who can," and the onslaught for the time was a failure. When day
broke on the battle-ground, nothing was to be
seen but a few fallen and mangled bodies, some
of them still breathing. But Grace's sense of
comparative security was sadly shaken, and
she felt that when the attack was again renewed on the Residency, she would be in the
very forefront of the battle. Nor was it only
or chiefly for herself that she feared. Should
her letter have miscarried, or should her father
miss the messengers, returning with the weak
force he had started with, he might run unconsciously into the arms of the enemy.
Nothing, indeed, was more likely; yet what
could she do but pray, and strive to hope?

CHAPTER XXXIX.

PRIZE OF WAR.

IT boots not to tell at length how Moray had
sped on his mission to the Sultan. The Scot,
with his great knowledge of the East, had at-
tained a success beyond his hopes, and had succeeded chiefly by showing himself in his natural
character. His manly bearing, his frank yet
courteous manners, the calm but keen glance
of the eye, the commanding dignity of his stalwart person, had all imposed on the Malay.
As we have seen, the Sultan had a considerable
personal interest in the prosperity of the English Company. Sure that the merchants could
never become his masters—he had never read
the history of the English in Hindustan—he
welcomed them as a counterpoise to the
Dutch, a power that was always to be dreaded.
After the death of Chamberlain, he had in-

clined to yield if he had not actually lent
himself to the intrigues that were being
actively pushed forward at his Court.   But
he hated and he feared those brothers of his
who fomented them, and distrusted and de-
spised the foreign adventurers with whom they
originated.   The arrival of Moray was a pleasure and a relief.   A quick judge of character,
a worshipper of strength, he saw at once that
he had to deal with a man, and that the reins
of administration at Sanga were to be tight-
ened in an iron grasp.   The Sultan delighted
to honour the Scotchman.   He sent him a
robe of honour; he offered him rich presents.
With the swift transition so common in oriental politics, the loyalists or Court party were
at once in the ascendant.   Warriors passed
over to it; the brothers of the Crown began to
think of making a bolt; and the adventurers,
who had fancied their game as good as won,
felt their heads sitting uncomfortably on their
shoulders.   Nor was Moray the man to neglect
his opportunities.   He had brought a supply
of money as well as gifts, and he distributed
both liberally but discreetly, so that after a
very few days, if there was a difficulty in the

situation, it was that the Pharaoh of Sarambang was loath to let him go. But by this
time Moray's footing had become so strong,
that he could speak to the Sultan with the
frankness of friendship. He told him that he
had left an unprotected daughter in circumstances which, to say the least, were somewhat
critical; and he pledged his honour that a
prompt departure would be followed by a
speedy return.

So the Sultan was persuaded by this diplo-
matist to act on the old Scotch saying, and
professed himself ready to speed his parting
guest. Had he needed help in the way of
war-galleys, Moray might have had it to any
extent. The nobles and the chiefs were only
too willing to form a war-squadron to take him
back in triumph. Moray was content with
the moral influence he had regained, and only
asked for one chief of rank as companion,
furnished with full powers as the Sultan's
accredited representative. Even had the necessity been more urgent, he would have
scrupled as to engaging a fleet of volunteers,
who might have insisted upon turning the expedition into a pleasure-party — *i.e.*, sacking

peaceful villages, and making curious collections of heads.

With his strong will and his tact, Moray had his way, and that without turning either his friends or his flatterers into secret enemies. He had named the noble Malay to be sent as his companion—a man in as high repute for honesty as for courage. Pangaran Jaffir had become the sworn brother-in-arms of the Scottish governor, the bond having been ratified by solemn ceremonial and mysterious religious rites. Thenceforward, he was to be counted upon for life or death. And Moray had special reasons for selecting him, inasmuch as he had had territory in the neighbourhood of Sanga, and still prided himself on some hereditary influence over the surrounding tribes.

So it was settled: the sailing had been fixed for the following day, and a grand feast of dismissal was being given at the palace the evening before the morning of departure. Everything had so far gone off well; and when the malt threatened to get above the meal, as they say in Scotland,—that is to say, when the banqueters began to warm with the flow of talk and the strong liquors,— Moray had suggested to the Sultan the propriety of retiring. He was in high spirits himself—all had gone so well with him : nor was he insensible to the evident respect and admiration of the gallant though wild chivalry that surrounded the board.

When of a sudden there came an interruption that startled the Sultan and his company, as the writing on the wall had scared Belshazzar on a similar occasion. A messenger of humble rank, in mean dress, and of travel-worn aspect, was seen standing at the bottom of the hall under the draped-back hangings. And there seemed likely to be a somewhat lively scene, as guards and revellers were talking of cutting him in pieces. When the Sultan rose in his outraged dignity, and claiming the rights of death or torture as a privilege of the Crown, commanded that the intruder should be brought before him. No sooner said than done; it seemed to be precisely what the messenger desired, for he carried himself with a strange fearlessness. He prostrated himself at the feet of the Sultan with every demonstration of respect, but he kept his eyes fixed on the white chief who sat by the Sultan's side. And to that white chief, after sundry phrases and explanations, was delivered the packet he drew from the bosom of his dress.

Notwithstanding the spread of cheap telegraphy, we have all experienced that it is nervous work opening telegrams under certain circumstances; and even letters delivered unexpectedly may be pregnant with acute anxiety. Moray was a strong man, but he was the fondest of fond fathers. The fears he had striven to lull to rest woke up simultaneously, like a nest of vipers suddenly laid bare to the sunshine. It was with trembling fingers he vainly tried to steady that he tore the packet open, sent by express from Sanga. It was strange, too, in the circumstances, to read " Glenconan, Ross-shire, N.B.," emblazoned on the pages. Grace had brought a supply of her wire-wove, cream-laid note-paper along with her. And as he read, his hands trembled more and more, and a mist came gathering over his eyes, though not before he had mastered the meaning of the contents. Then he called the hard training of a lifetime to his help, and with a mighty effort he mastered himself. Everything now depended — and how much it was !—on coolness, energy, and unflinching resolution. He laid the case before the Sultan, stating the facts concisely. The potentate was already willing to assist him, and he could hardly have been spoken to in a more happy hour. He was delighted to give a proof of the authority he had re-established by an appeal to the warriors assembled around him. As for Moray, under the pressure of the crisis, of course he cast all his scruples to the winds. He would carry a sufficient force along with him, and those who had provoked the onslaught must stand the consequences.

It was the Sultan of Sarambang in person who made the appeal to his martial following. The white chief of Sanga was to put to sea on a war expedition ; who would volunteer to form part of his fleet ? The hostile tribes from the eastward were threatening a descent on Sarambang territory : there was glory to be won, there might be booty to be regained ; unquestionably there was a deal of fighting to be done. Even in the cool, or rather the tropical heat of the morning, the appeal would have been received with enthusiasm. Now, the enthusiasm rose to frenzy, and the hall rang with acclamations. The scene might have reminded one of the preaching of a Christian crusade to fighting fanatics of the dark ages; of the gathering in some Highland chieftain's hall, before the circuit of the fiery cross and the clansmen taking the field. The Highland heart of Moray warmed to these wild tribesmen, and the warlike spirit of his forefathers blazed up in his breast. He struck the iron while it was hot; he spoke to them; they understood his gestures, if not his words; and he had only to pick and choose among the company. In making his choice he was helped by circumstances. He would put to sea as soon after daybreak as possible; and only those whose prahus were in readiness could go. The others who cared to come might follow at their leisure; and, in fact, it would be a case of " devil take the hindmost."

But as the Malay States have no Boards of Admiralty, seaworthy fleets may be despatched with startling rapidity. The prahus were lying moored off the shore, or dragged high and dry on the beach; the men, who

were scattered through the town, had only to
be wakened from their slumbers; the arms of
each amphibious warrior were ready to his
hand; and as for sea-stores, some provisions
were pitched into the boats, and for the rest,
the crews were ready to trust to their Providence or the prospects of pillage. Through
the short hours of the darkness that remained,
lights were seen flitting about in every direction; to the spectator looking down upon the
place from the crests of the hills in the back-
ground, it might have seemed to be invaded
by a plague of fire-flies. When the sunrise
was breaking over the sea in a blaze of golden
and crimson splendour, it gilded the swelling
sails of a gallant fleet, standing to the westward before favouring breezes.

For four-and-twenty hours all went well;
already, stretching across a width of bay to a
long projecting promontory, they had opened
the amphitheatre of volcanic mountains that
embraces the delta of the Sanga. Spite of
his self-command, Moray's heart had been
beating more and more violently, with quick
alternations of hopes and fears; yet he felt
that, with so much in his favour as yet, he

had every reason to be hopeful,—when all at once, the aspect of the weather changed; the favouring breezes fell and died away— the sultry air became intolerably oppressive. He saw the old pilot casting anxious glances towards the east, where heavy banks of cloud were darkening the horizon. The order was given to furl the flapping sails; and the men, settling down to the sweeps, still made steady progress. But the storm we have seen bursting over Sanga was gathering fast; and it is one thing to look at these tropical terrors from a bungalow, but quite another to face them on the open sea. The storm broke; but the seamen cared little for the peals of the thunder, nor yet for the fierce flashes of the lightning. They had more immediate cause for anxiety in the fitful gusts of the winds, broken loose upon them from three points of the compass; sinking as suddenly as they rose, and coming in a capricious succession of surprises. Away to their right was a sea, beginning to be lashed into raging surf, and to break in boiling billows. To the left were the perilous shallows, along a coast that was fringed with a jungle of impervious mangrove. And superstition came to heighten the horrors of the scene. In the darkening of what ought to have been broad day, there was a ghastly illumination of the crests of the breakers; and lurid flashes of fitful light seemed to rise out of the depths of the ocean. Balls of spectral fires, bred out of the ever-thickening darkness, gathered at the ends of the tapering yards and on the tips of the swaying masts. The rowers still bent to the sweeps; but the cadence of their chants died away, as their pulling became listless and irregular.

Then, when they were half-paralysed by superstitious apprehension, came the wild stress of the cylone. In five short minutes the fleet was scattered; each prahu whirled round by the irresistible blast in its own turmoil of mad wind and seething water. The cylone swept onwards swiftly as it had come; two or three stout craft had gone to the bottom, though, as all the Malays swim like ducks, most of the men had been picked up by other boats. Some of the prahus were scudding out to sea, like frightened and crippled sea-birds that had lost their heads; while others, following more dangerous instincts, had headed for the shallows, to beach themselves on any terms. Several still stuck to the commander-in-chief, though rather by chance than from any settled determination.

As for Moray, his heart had sunk, with what would have been the fall in the barometer, had his back carried such an instrument; but it was only because he feared that the storms in their courses were fighting against the salvation of his child. His heart had sunk, but his courage rose; and men who sought to read their fate in his face became reassured by his undaunted and impassible demeanour. The cylone had passed, but it was still blowing half a gale, and a surf, lashed up into fury, was raging and rolling towards a lee shore. Moray's prahu, still keeping the lead, had resumed its course, and held it like grim death. Food and drink had been served out to the drenched rowers, and the native officers, unwilling to show less courage than the white chief, had encouraged the crew by words and example. There is no braver race than that of these

Malays of Sumatra : no men are more indifferent to death. Nor has the world seen
any more daring seamen since the Vikings
of the north settled down and became civilised.
So the shattered relics of the scattered flotilla
were still holding on in their course for Sanga.

But the wind had changed with the cyclone,
and was setting steadily in their faces. Even
by dint of desperate pulling they made but
slow way, and many a weary hour had dragged
by ere they cleared the last of the headlands
and sighted the *embouchure* of the Sanga
River. The seething bar was not the only
obstacle they saw before them ; and indeed,
as the bar had been protected from the pre-
vailing wind, it was less angry than might
have been expected. The only thing that
Moray did see, after the first glance, was a
fleet of prahus advancing pleasantly from the
opposite direction. Then the pirates were a
reality : they had drifted apparently in place
of being driven ; and, in any case, they num-
bered at least three times his force, and so
effectually sealed the entrance to the Sanga.
Had a weaker man found himself in a similar
situation, he would have appealed to the head-

long courage of his followers, and endeavoured
to force a passage at all hazards.   Moray
weighed the circumstances, and acknowledged
that the attempt would be desperate.   The
best thing that could be done was to take
counsel deliberately, and he had an admirable
counsellor at his elbow.   He signalled to Pangaran Jaffir, who was following in his wake,
and in another moment that chief was alongside.   All the Malay's hereditary animosities
were roused by the sight of feudal enemies
who must have ravaged his territory frequently
before.   But being a veteran warrior, eager as
he was to strike them, he preferred to make
sure before he struck.   Knowing the " lie of
the land," and having grasped the situation,
he had a plan of operations cut and dried.
He had people with him who knew a path
used by the crews of fishing-boats, which led
to a village in the jungle.   From that village
there were woodland paths, which debouched
upon Sanga in the vicinity of the Residency ;
and by following them, if Moray did not anticipate the pirates, at all events he might
hope to deliver the attack before they had
done any great mischief.

The plan was no sooner suggested than decided upon. Moray's little squadron ostentatiously backed water and beat a retreat, to the great glorification of the enemy, who had been observing them. As they drew back behind cover of the headland, they heard the clamour of shouts and of drums beaten in triumph. "He laughs best who laughs last," soliloquised Moray grimly, as, full of fears and hopes, he pressed forward the disembarkation.

There were others who were watching the approach of the piratical fleet with interest nearly as intense. The barbarous levies that beset the settlement welcomed the approach of their ferocious allies; while Matusin was in presence of an onslaught he could hardly hope to withstand. He had marked, too, the advance of the prahus from the opposite direction, and when he saw them withdraw, he had been more disheartened than surprised. It would have been nothing less than madness to face the force opposed to them. All the same, in bitterness of spirit, and in an interview which Grace had sought with him, he had said something of broken pledges and of the Resident failing them at need. Then

Grace had flashed out, and seldom had an out-
break of temper been better timed.

"My father is with these men ; and he will
either die or cut his way to us. If he could
turn his back on his only daughter, he would
never fail the followers who look to him for
support."

I do not pretend to say that even the quick-
witted Malay could follow Miss Moray's exact
words. But even better than by the translation attempted by her handmaiden, it was
emphasised by the girl's eyes and indignant
attitude. He knew he was being pushed hard
to the wall ; he was determined to sell his life
dearly if he must part with it ; and he turned
to the chiefs and the head-men who surrounded him. He told them that the white
leader was at hand, and coming to their help ;
his daughter, who was in mysterious communication with her father, knew it ; and if
they set manfully about the defence, they
might make sure of a speedy deliverance. In
fact, his address was a free reading of the
maxim, that the gods help those who help
themselves ; and he spoke to men who held
their lives so cheaply, that with that super-

stitious encouragement they became positively
reckless. The strategy of the Malays was
simple enough. They must fall back on the
defence of the town, and make good the
stockades. Matusin would gladly have met
the assailing flotilla in the river; but with
his weakened forces and the few prahus at
his disposal, that was altogether out of the
question.

As with the war of the elements the day
before, there was a lull and a breathing-time
before the storm burst. The pirates probably
spent it in communicating with their friends
on shore, and combining some plan of operations that might carry the defences with a
rush. As for the defenders, they had been
dismissed to their posts, where they seemed
likely to be awkwardly embarrassed by the
frightened women who clung to them.

At the Residency, if there was extreme excitement, there was comparative calm. There
were Malay guards, but the gates had been
closed against intruders; and the few Europeans had no families to care for them. Then
Grace, rising to the emergency, had been here,
there, and everywhere. If there were cowards

within the precincts, it was difficult to show timidity before the beautiful young woman so heroically serene. A Jeanne d'Arc, whether medieval or modern, is a mighty influence in circumstances of the kind ; and if Grace was carrying herself so resolutely in public, it was because she had risen from her knees only the moment before.

Mr Rafferty was likewise religious after his fashion, but he only crossed himself and invoked the saints, in such appalling circumstances as the storm. Now, in his anxiety for the big fight to begin, he was restless, like the sea-birds before a hurricane. He was ready to talk to anybody who would listen, and vague fancies of scientific warfare were floating in his excited brain. So he joined Miss Moray, who had gone up to her watch-tower, and was looking wistfully down the river at the blockading war-boats.

"Thim pirates are taking it remarkably aisy, Miss ; bad luck to them," remarked Mr Rafferty, respectfully, by way of opening the conversation. "It's a pity but we could send thim down a few fire-ships or some half-dozen of tarpadoes by way of an agreeable surprise."

Grace started: the idea seemed a good one: the difficulty was the impossibility of realising it, and half unconsciously she shook her head.

"Of course it's out of the question," continued Mr Rafferty, in answer; "for Mathieson and his benighted savages have none of the materials at hand. But divil a one of me would ask betther spoort than to see the boats in a blaze, and the beggars on board of thim swimming for their lives."

There were no torpedoes, it was true: there were neither the men nor the materials for a despatch of fire-boats; yet, looking at the situation not in the light of sport, but very seriously, it struck Grace that there might be something in Rafferty's notion. With searching glances she embraced the scene before her eyes, and then she commanded Rafferty to guide her to Matusin. The restless Irishman asked nothing better; and, though mortally curious, he had the discretion to ask no questions. Grace at that moment had something of her father's look when at his sternest; her knitted eyebrows and her compressed lips repressed all familiarity, and forwardness stood abashed before dignity.

If the Malay chief was in any way put out by the English girl's proposal, it was only that it had not occurred to himself, being so entirely in accordance with the traditions of Malay bush-fighting.

"The day is drawing on," Grace had begun, looking upwards towards the sloping sun; "your enemies will scarcely attack you before morning."

The Malay would not commit himself, but seemed inclined to agree. Then Grace broached a scheme, which Rafferty's crude idea had suggested. The pirates had brought up at a point where the estuary was closing rapidly into the deep, narrow channel of the river. Their boats had let down their anchors or lashed themselves to trees on the banks; one way or another, in their overweening confidence, they were crowded, hampered, and careless. On either side of the river stretched the forest, with the dense undergrowth dried up into tinder after the prolonged drought, for the sultriness and the sunshine had already licked up the deluge that had fallen the day before. And the wind, if it came in gusts, was still setting steadily from the eastward.

"Why," said Grace, "should you not wait
for the dusk, and then set a light to the
jungle? If the fire does nothing else, it will
delay the attack, and the hours we gain are
everything, when my father and his people
are outside there."

Matusin being half a savage, and having
life and property at stake, swallowed down
any feelings of petty jealousy. Gallantly he
sank on one knee to kiss the hand of the fair
counsellor, and then begged permission to
withdraw to make the arrangements for the
conflagration. And when Grace had thanked
Rafferty for the idea she had utilised, the
Irishman only asked, by way of recompense,
that the young lady would "hurry back to
the Residency, and lave him free to go with
the niggers, and superinthend."

If the pirates kept watch and ward at all,
it was on the side of the settlement they were
threatening. But, in fact, there was little
discipline or order, and each man did as seemed
right in his own eyes. In short, they had
sold the hide of the bear they meant to hunt
and kill on the morrow. Some were feasting,
singing, and carousing; others were sleeping

the sleep of the oblivious, through a din that might have wakened the Seven Sleepers. On some boats the fires were blazing up, or had smouldered down among cinders in the braziers; in others, the fires had gone out altogether. Here there would be a patch of blinding glare; here the moonshine was softly silvering the water; and there there was utter darkness, beneath the black shadows of the trees.

Had there been watchers placed in the stillness of the night, the first warning would have been in the shape of a faint crackling. As it was, thanks to the noise, no one lent an ear to that admonition; while, owing to the mingled glare of the fires with the moonshine, that partially illuminated the fleet, no one detected a sporadic glimmering among the trees, like the lights of some scores of gigantic glowworms. But the fires had been kindled close at hand and in many places, and they spread and blazed up with marvellous rapidity. One minute the fleet was either mad with revelry or sunk in slumber; the next, each soul on board was on foot, and face to face with an appalling catastrophe. The flames that were roaring up the great stems of the trees, finding fuel in the luxuriant growth of the creepers, were leaping from branch to branch overhead, and darkening the skies above the glare with the smoke from an infernal illumination. The flames twisted themselves serpent - like round each pendant festoon and drooping withe till they sputtered and went out in the current of the river that rippled in streams of blood, as it ran by in the crimson glow. And through the red blaze and the rising roar came the shrill shrieks of the monkeys and other miserable animals being consumed—had anybody had ears to hear them. Had Matusin been a born leader instead of being merely a quick-witted warrior, he would have contrived an attack on the fleet for that moment, and turned the panic into an overwhelming disaster. But having failed to contemplate probabilities, or to count the chances, he was only looking on from a distance, rubbing his hands, and congratulating himself. Nor did he even take the necessary precautions to regulate the course of the flames he had kindled.

The pirates, horror-stricken and taken by surprise, were left to save themselves as they could. In the instincts of self-preservation, there was no lack of activity. Lithe figures, stripped nearly to the skin, were observed bounding about in the reflections of the fires, dragging at anchors or hauling at ropes. Prahu after prahu was seen to push out from " the ruck," the crews getting to the sweeps, as they floated themselves clear on the current. One or two of the boats were abandoned, that had been lashed too securely to the blazing trees. But on the whole, the assailing squadron had been rather frightened than hurt. Not a few of the craft showed like moths that had singed their wings at a candle. Not a few of the crews were burned, as a very great many were scorched. But as the men of all these amphibious fighting races can swim like sharks, no one perished in the water who had not been crippled by the fire. And so the scared and scattered fleet assembled and came to anchor again, in a little bay immediately within the bar.

Matusin had scored the trick and might have won the game, had he boldly played out his trumps. As it was, he left his discomfited adversaries free to take their re-

venge ; and when they sent their scouts out
to reconnoitre, they found that the fire had
been by no means an unmixed misfortune to
them.   Matusin had kindled his firebrands in
a sense of absolute security.   A broad belt of
thin orchards and cultivated ground separated
the dense jungle from the settlement.   He
had, perhaps, forgotten the fringe of trees
that ran along the bank of the river ; but
that fringe, feeding the fires, had conducted
them along to the stockades.   A breadth of a
score of yards or more had been consumed,
or charred ; and the scouts, slipping back to
the chiefs who sent them, had reported a
practicable breach.   As for the garrison, in
their intoxication over the discomfiture of
their enemies, they thought of nothing in the
meantime but rejoicings and congratulations.
They knew that the watchful assailants in the
bush would be in consternation at the disaster
to their allies.

When they least expected it, they had a
disagreeable awakening.   The enemy they believed to be demoralised was seen coming up
the river again, with all the impulsion of
double-banked sets of oars, smarting from re-

cent fright and bodily injuries, and animated by the assurance of a speedy revenge. While the leading prahus swept up the river, facing the desultory fire of the field-pieces in the works, a body of warriors, flung quickly ashore, hurled themselves forward on the enfeebled stockades. The charred stakes were shivered before their rush like pasteboard; the defenders fell at their posts, or sought safety in flight; the allies in the woods, with answering yells, came swarming over the palisades; and before any serious resistance was even begun, the settlement had been virtually carried. The rush on the Residency from the river-side was irresistible. There, again, the Malays on guard were either speared or cut to pieces or scattered. The terrible *krises* made deadly play. The few Europeans, according to their temperaments, either resisted or cried for quarter: not that it made much difference how they behaved, since the brave man and the coward met a common fate. Poor Rafferty, who had scented the battle from afar like Job's war-horse, was naturally one of the first to be knocked upon the head; and as for the lady for whom he would have given his life, her fate, although she was merely a prisoner, seemed hardly preferable to his. Swooning and in despair, now that the worst had come, just as she had been giving heartfelt thanks for an almost miraculous deliverance, Grace was carried in the arms of triumphant barbarians on board the galley of the piratical leader.

CHAPTER XL.

THE SACK OF SANGA.

MORAY'S idea was naturally to get his little forces together and go straight to the rescue of his daughter. But Pangaran Jaffir opposed plausible arguments and a passive resistance not to be overcome. He urged that as yet they were so few in number, the venture must be doubtful or even desperate, considering that, before they reached the settlement, they might have to make a running fight of it through the jungle. It was most unlikely that the enemy would make the attack that evening, and if they did risk it, they would certainly be repulsed. Meantime they themselves would be hourly gaining reinforcements; for already several of the prahus of their scattered fleet could be seen coming up behind. Finally, neither he nor any of his people would undertake to guide the advance, at the risk of going astray and being benighted. The Malay, bold as a lion in daylight, was by no means proof against the terrors of the forest in the darkness, especially after his superstition had been awakened in the horrors of the recent storm.

Moray gnashed his teeth, but resigned himself. There was truth, after all, in what the Malay said, and he believed that Sanga could not be carried except after hard fighting. For that evening, at least, it was surely safe, and his relieving party on the morrow would have manifold chances in its favour. So, lighting their fires, the Sarambang men bivouacked on a strip of shingly beach, where now and again they welcomed the arrival of the stragglers. There was no merriment or carousing, as on board of the hostile fleet : the men were weary with the work, and far from being in good spirits. Moray saw that even could he have persuaded them to advance, he could have hoped to accomplish little with such followers.

He had lain down and tried hard to sleep. He was weary like the others with the double

strain on mind and body, and he needed rest
for the morrow. But rest would not come at
his call. He turned and tossed, with the
flames of the watch-fires dancing before his
eyes, till the swarthy figures that from time to
time flitted across them seemed like so many
restless fiends to his distempered senses. He
felt gloomy forebodings he could too easily explain, and it was scarcely a relief to rise and
pace the beach, looking out through the calm
silence of the night on the twinkling heavens
and the tossing sea. Naturally his eyes were
directed towards Sanga, for there was the load-
stone that attracted his thoughts. When suddenly he rubbed those aching eyes of his, and
stood gazing with fixed attention. A faint,
ruddy gleam was streaking the sky above the
tops of the forest-trees. He fancied at first it
might be the flashing of sheet-lightning, but
it was too steady for that. It brightened, it
reddened, and quickly extended itself, till it
spanned the horizon in a fiery arch, quenching
those twinkling stars in its blaze, and darkening with clouds of smoke the deep azure of
the heavens. It was the glare of a great conflagration, hanging over the site of the settle-

ment.   Assuredly Sanga was being sacked,
and—his daughter !—his daughter !

Moray was neither the man nor in the mood
to stand like Lord Ullin, wringing his hands
and lamenting.   There was no waste of wild
water before him—only a broad belt of jungle,
with foot-tracks that were known to lead
through it.   In a dozen of strides, or rather of
bounds, the old deerstalker was standing over
the Malay chief, shaking him by the shoulder.
One touch would have sufficed.   In a second
Pangaran Jaffir was on his legs ; in a second
or two more, he had all his wits about him.
Moray had meant to command or to press immediate action.   But there was no need.   The
swarthy Malay, in spite of the hue of the skin,
sympathised with the white chieftain and
father.   His chivalry was enlisted : his manhood was in question ; and whether he had
reposed himself with an hour or two of sleep
or not, his superstitious tremors had been dis-
sipated.   Rather to forearm the friend of his
Sultan against casualties than for any other
reason, he warned or reminded him that it was
no easy matter to grope their way through
thick jungle in the darkness.   The guides had

but vague recollections of the localities, which might be beset by bands of ambushed warriors familiar with them. But so much said, he gave his orders peremptorily, and in ten minutes the whole of the party was on foot, and in readiness to follow their leaders. If there were still fear or reluctance, the boldest did not dare give a sign of it. Pangaran had a hot temper and a heavy hand.

But "the more haste, the worse speed," is a time-honoured proverb that is very true; and so Moray found to his cost. It was tedious work and frightfully aggravating, leading weary if not unwilling men through a gloomy labyrinth of winding wood-tracks. To be sure they were never going very far wrong, for each false path soon ended in a cul-de-sac. To be sure they could steer their course by the conflagration, which threw a fixed beacon-light from the goal of the march, whenever they came into low scrub or a clearing. But reluctant and dispirited men began to drag their limbs more and more painfully; and the spirits sank with the failing flesh. The self-possessed Moray was wellnigh maddened. Suspense was being

strained, till it became almost intolerable;
he felt inclined to cast himself down under
a bush in despair, like the Israelitish prophet
in the wilderness; and yet, for the life and
honour of his daughter, he dare not break
down. All depended on his keeping up his
courage; the tremblers who followed must
draw encouragement from him, if they were
to be ready to show themselves men with
the daybreak. His great comfort was in the
bearing of Pangaran Jaffir. That veteran
warrior stepped out like a lad; he had entirely recovered his shaken nerve, and showed
the counsel in moments of difficulty of a
bush-fighter of ripe experience. And in
strange contrast to his domineering demeanour to his men, he won Moray's most cordial
gratitude by silent but eloquent expressions
of sympathy. More than once in the darkness he clasped the Scotchman's hand, or laid
a light touch of cheerful consolation on his
shoulder. It might have seemed matter of
thankfulness that they had no fighting to
face: a sudden attack upon their files in
the dark must have begun with a panic
and ended in a massacre. But that Moray

took for a melancholy sign, and as they still groped their way unopposed, his heart felt heavier and heavier. They surprised a forest-hamlet with its women and children, but they neither cared nor needed to stop and ask questions. The men must have gone forward to the sack of Sanga, where the vultures of the woods were gathering to the carnage.

The more haste, the worse speed; and the sun had already risen over the opposite trees before they saw the glimmerings of daylight through the thinning skirts of the jungle. Father as he was, Moray had enough of the sage and the soldier in him to consent to call a halt to dress the column, while scouts were sent creeping forward. The scouts came back with the astounding report that there were no signs of a fire in the settlement. They had gone no farther than the stockades behind the Residency. The defences were apparently without defenders; but the roof and walls of the Residency and other houses seemed intact.

Tossed about with violent revulsions of feeling, now hoping and now despairing, the cool

Glenconan was no longer to be restrained. Like one of his young Highland deer-hounds slipped on the slot of the wounded deer, he would have flung himself on the horns of a stag at bay. Pangaran Jaffir did not attempt to hold him back; indeed his old blood and his warlike ardour were already both at the boiling-point. The men now quickly rallied and mustered in loose order beneath the open fringe of the forest : there was a rush, in which they took the stockades in their stride; they crossed the enclosures of the Residency at a run, with its master still well to the front, and they burst through its unprotected windows and doors, some of them swarming up the pillars of the verandahs.

Hangings had been torn down and the furniture wrecked. Lighter articles of any value had been swept away, with a cleanness and celerity that would have done honour to the myrmidons of a London cheap broker. The storm had passed everywhere and shattered everything; and on the other side of the house, where resistance had been made, corpses were strewed over the lawn and through the flowers.

The distracted father searched everywhere; he hunted high and low, and all in vain. Grace's little sitting-room and her bedroom had been rudely violated like the rest; only from under a fallen mosquito-net crawled poor Finette, piteously moaning, and badly wounded by the thrust of a Malay *kris*. It was touching to see the poor dog cheer up at the sight of her master; drag herself along the floor to his feet, and cover his hands with her caresses. And Moray was touched: it was no shame to his manhood that he caught her up in his arms, and covered her with his kisses. But unhappily the dog, which did all but speak, could tell him nothing of her mistress. So he set her gently down again, dropped from the window on to the ground, and hurried after his followers into the gardens to pursue his investigations.

A shout drew him away to a clump of shrubbery. As chance would have it, it was the very thicket where Rafferty had ensconced himself on the eventful evening when he sought his interview with Grace. And there lay poor Mr Rafferty again, but on this occasion quite unable to bestir himself. Indeed, as he said subsequently, it was only by a miracle, and by virtue of the blessed crucifix he always wore next to his skin, that the life of the hard-fighting Irishman had been spared. Be that as it may, he had simply been "kilt," in other words, he had merely had his head broken,—with a chance wound in the chest, "that counted little one way or the other,"— and then had been tumbled into the thicket. Now, being picked up by "thim friendly niggers," he dragged himself on to one elbow and tried to "spake." But it was not till the sight of the Resident made it worth while, that he strove to string some articulate sentences together; nor did he succeed in making himself intelligible till after an internal application of spirits. Impatient as he was, Moray had held back his flask; *arrack* seemed hardly to be the thing for a wounded European in the circumstances. But Rafferty made an effort, seized it, swallowed, and delivered himself—

"Sure it's the finest medicine in the world, and it goes down like mother's milk. For now," he added, recalling his temperance pledge with a dreamy sigh, "I'm free from my promise." Then remembering what had passed, in his weakness he fairly broke down. At last Moray did prevail on him to speak, though the thought of the pain he was involuntarily inflicting nearly gave the warm-hearted Irishman a relapse. The house had been taken from the other side when he was making a fight of it in the verandah looking seaward. The last thing he had seen of Miss Grace, she was being carried to the river in the arms of a big barbarian. He had made a dash to the rescue, "but they were too many for me—bad luck to them. They knocked me flat on my back here, and I saw no more till ye wakened me. But you'll be going after her, sir, and you'll take me with you," added Mr Rafferty. "You can lay me down in the bottom of one of the boats till I'm wanted; and anyhow, when the fighting begins, you may trust Jack Rafferty to come up to time."

Mr Rafferty's request, mad as it was, served the purpose of rousing Moray from his stupefaction. His child was gone; the settlement was seemingly evacuated by the enemy; whatever the chances, there was nothing for it but to take up the chase, without unnecessarily losing one moment. But it was his

destiny in those two dismal days to have his
patience strained almost beyond the endurable.
This man, who had prided himself upon cool
self-control, was perpetually breaking his teeth
against obstacles nearly insurmountable. Matusin was dead or had disappeared, and the
survivors of the garrison had vanished with
him. As for the followers of Pangaran Jaffir,
they had scattered themselves about through
the town in search of any stray articles to
plunder; and the boats they were accustomed
to man were left in the bay beyond the forest.
Before he could lay hands on Pangaran, before
that chief could get the body of his people
together again, much invaluable time had been
wasted. Even then, with the scratch crews of
strangers assembled round the Sanga prahus,
it was hard work getting a flotilla to sea.
The Sarambang people objected to being taken
away from the joys of pillaging, and they
knew, besides, that they were terribly over-
matched, should the enemy be inclined to
shorten sail and offer battle. Even Pangaran
—and not unnaturally in the circumstances—
gave the order for embarkation much against
his will. His common-sense told him that if

he were not going to sea on a wild-goose chase, he was staking life and reputation against desperate odds. Hours had gone by before the boats were hastily supplied with some provisions and water; and if the start was effected at last, Moray saw only too plainly that it was because the crews were encouraged by the thought that a stern chase is a long chase, especially when the chased is the stronger, and has practically unlimited law.

CHAPTER XLI.

THE RESCUE.

WE left Ralph Leslie at Penang, in a reaction of anxieties after his first relief. It was no easy matter the getting a cast on board ship to the Sumatra coast, and even chartering a craft on his own account was more than a question of time and money. The mongrel skippers in these seas had a wholesome dread of a neighbourhood where pirates were wont to be as common as lighthouses are rare. The 'Sir Stamford Scraper' was still under repair, and the master declined the responsibility of doing more than detaching a veteran of the crew to accompany Mr Leslie as pilot. It really seemed that he was likely to be indefinitely leg-bound, in which case he must have fretted himself off with a fever or a liver complaint— when fortune very seasonably befriended him.

H.M.S. Severn, a big composite gun-vessel, carrying four heavy breech-loading guns, with a couple of Gardner machine-guns to boot, was signalled, and soon steamed into the port. Naturally the captain was invited to dine at Government House, and there Leslie met him. It immediately occurred to our friend that all his ends would be more than answered if he could only take the Severn to Sanga. He had spoken on the subject to the Governor, who doubted whether the business could be managed, but was very willing to help it forward. But when they broached the affair to Captain MacDonald after the claret had been circulating, he made no difficulties; quite the contrary. As it chanced, he had met Moray and his daughter in London; a Celt himself, his heart warmed to a Highlander in difficulties, and, like the Malay chiefs, his chivalry was enlisted on behalf of a fair maiden in distress. He was a strong-willed officer besides, with influence at the Admiralty; and moreover, he fancied the idea of a flying trip to Sumatra, with an off-chance of a little fighting thrown in.

"Sumatra lies beyond my roving commis-

sion," he said, " and I cannot act without
definite orders. The admiral on the station
is at sea with the squadron—Heaven only
knows where !—and I can't communicate with
him. But I'll tell you what I'll do. I'll send
a telegram off to the Admiralty, asking leave
and pleading urgency. I don't doubt I shall
get leave ; but to make matters doubly sure,
perhaps the Governor will back me up with
the Foreign Office."

The Governor was agreeable, and Leslie
said, moreover, that Moray had a nephew,
an active M.P., who would undertake to focus
the influence of the President of the Council
on the affair.

" Then I think we may consider it as good
as settled," exclaimed the gallant skipper, rubbing his hands. " I shall be ready to heave
up the anchor at a moment's notice, and, Mr
Leslie, you had better bring your traps on
board."

So, to cut the story short, the three telegrams were despatched ; the answers were
altogether satisfactory, and the Severn spread
her canvas to a favouring breeze, while the
stokers and auxiliary screw lent a second set

of wings to her flight. She had sighted the volcanic peaks behind Sanga, looming like light-grey clouds on the southern horizon. Gradually the forests had been seen, rising slowly out of the sea; and then they could distinguish through the glasses the verdant patches of clearing on the slopes behind the black shore-belt of the mangroves. It struck them as singular that there was something looking like a haze of smoke just where, according to the charts, should be the mouth of the Sanga river.

"It seems as if they had been burning forest," remarked Captain MacDonald, passing the telescope to his first lieutenant.

"It's a forest-fire, and a big one too, sure enough, sir," returned that officer, after a long steady gaze. "Strange that they should be burning forest, too, and to that extent, and at this time, if that be the river that leads to the settlement."

Leslie, who was standing at the captain's elbow, took the alarm at once. In the excitement of his approach to the girl he loved so dearly, his apprehensions were ready to forebode the worst. Yet he dropped the glass he had seized, as a hail came down from the crosstrees.

"A fleet of boats standing eastward under the shore, three points away on the lee bow."

In a minute or so Leslie, with much resolution, though with little grace or dexterity, had accomplished his first ascent on board ship, and was holding on somehow to the stays by the side of the look-out man in the main-top. The captain, sympathising with the natural anxiety of his friend and passenger, had put his dignity in his pocket, and followed. Leslie, by something like an intuition, had more than a glimmering of the truth; but the captain shook his head when it was proposed that he should overhaul those flying prahus.

"They may be from Sanga, or they may be on peaceful business; and very possibly they are. If we overhauled them, they would run into shallow water; and it would be more than my commission is worth to attack them, without knowing how the land lies. You are making yourself needlessly uneasy, believe me, my dear fellow; and in any case, the only thing to be done is to drive hard ahead and communicate with the settlement. Then, if we find that those gentry ought to be overhauled for any reason, rely upon it I shall be alongside of them in no time."

Ralph saw the reason of the thing, and was forced to be content. Fresh fuel was heaped on the furnaces; and the Severn, bending over, cut through the waves at a pace that would have contented any one but a half-frenzied lover.

But like the Hebrew watchman who saw the swift messengers, the look-out man in the Severn had his work cut out for him.

"A boat crossing the bar," was the next announcement from on high; "another"—"four"—"six"—"thirteen."

"A second flotilla," exclaimed the captain; "the plot thickens. But I shall speak those latter gentry at any rate, Mr Leslie; and in fifty minutes or so at the outside, I hope your mind may be set at rest."

This squadron at all events was friendly. It made no attempt to escape her Majesty's war-ship. On the contrary, one of the biggest of the prahus was rapidly rowed towards the Severn; and ere long, and standing out on the lofty prow, Ralph distinguished the figure

of his uncle.   A strange meeting in such circumstances, in those tropical seas!   The ship
furled her upper canvas and reversed her en-
gines; the prahu was swept adroitly alongside,
and Moray, seizing the side-ropes, swung himself up upon the deck.

Each fibre in his nerves was throbbing; he
stood there like the high-mettled racer, among
the score of competitors eager for the start,
with self-control as a rider, reining him in.
He first grasped his nephew's hand, and exclaimed, "The captain?"   Leslie, only too
ready to take the alarm, had no time to speak,
for Captain MacDonald stepped forward, courteous but silent.   He saw that seconds were
precious, and that it was for the Resident at
Sanga to speak.   The father told his tale in
few words; but before he had well finished,
the order had been given to change the course
of the Severn.   Then there was leisure to
listen to a more detailed account of events,
as each yard of canvas that had been reefed
was spread again to the light breeze; while
engineers and stokers, thrilling in sympathy,
were feeding the furnaces and poking the
fires.   The fact had somehow speedily got

wind that the beautiful daughter of their stout old countryman was being carried away by those ruffianly Malays, who were melting out of sight on the eastern horizon; and each British seaman felt a personal longing to bring the rascally ravishers to book.

Captain MacDonald, when his own kind-hearted curiosity was satisfied, with the tact and sympathy of a gentleman, left the uncle and nephew to themselves. His delicacy, if not misplaced, was needless. Their minds were preoccupied with one terrible idea: they said nothing that all the world might not have heard. At all events, they might be pretty easy upon one point: the Severn was swiftly overhauling the flying squadron; in a couple of hours at the utmost she would have it under her guns. What might happen then, Heaven only could tell. Old Malay mariners, who had come aboard with Moray, declared that all along that coast the mangrove jungle was impervious—that there was no possibility of the enemy beaching their boats and beating a retreat by land. But, on the other hand, the sea shallowed so gradually—though they did not profess to report accurate soundings

—that it was very possible the piratical squadron might keep beyond reach of the corvette.

So it proved. The Severn cut off the retreat, as it would have taken its natural course round a jutting sand-spit: the Malay squadron was baffled and embayed, but at the same time it brought to in comparative safety. Captain MacDonald, though in the habit of acting for himself, called a war-council on his quarter-deck under these critical circumstances. Or rather, he consulted his two civilian passengers, who had all that was most dear in their lives at stake.

"In other circumstances, I should cannonade the scoundrels," said the captain, "and then pipe away the boats' crews and send them to attack under cover of the guns. But——"

"For God's sake, don't use the guns, Captain MacDonald!" exclaimed the unfortunate father. Then, recollecting himself, he added with an effort, "And yet you must do your duty."

"They have sacked an English settlement," returned the captain, "and doubtless it is my duty to attack at any cost, and to use all available means. Well, —— it all, duty must go to the wall for once. We must attack, I suppose; but whatever it may cost the ship's company, I won't run the chance of harming a hair of your daughter's head. We might blockade them, to be sure, barring changes in the weather, and possibly bring them to terms; and yet I greatly doubt whether, under the circumstances, anything would justify me in letting them go free."

Moray hesitated for a moment; then spoke with determination,—

"No British officer could do so; and were I weak enough and base enough to make such a request to you, in your place I could only refuse. But I know those Malays, and if you reduce them to despair by blockading, with the choice between surrender and starvation, they are capable of devising any revenge on their captives. There is but one thing to be done, and we must leave the consequences to a merciful God. If you are willing to send your boats to the attack, get to work without wasting a moment. And God knows how bitterly I regret that, on our account, your brave fellows should have to fight under any disadvantage."

" Chances of war and of the service, my dear sir. I answer for them, that not a man will waste a thought upon that. I am only sorry that duty compels me to remain on board, and that I must hand over the honour and the glory of the rescue to my first lieutenant."

His first lieutenant was far from sharing his regrets. Scarcely had the boatswain's whistle resounded along the decks, than the boats were swinging from the davits, and balancing themselves on the surface of the water. The crews had tumbled over the sides, the men had seized upon the oars, marines and supernumerary blue-jackets had stowed themselves away in their places, and ranging rapidly in line, or rather in crescent of battle, the little squadron swept swiftly towards the shore.

The steam-launch led the way in the centre, carrying Leslie, Moray, and some of his Malays as passengers. The pirate flotilla, at anchor in an irregular line, opened a heavy though desultory fire as the English approached.

Showers of bullets from antiquated rifles and muskets were mingled with flights of arrows. Gongs were violently beaten, wild war-cries resounded along the waves; there was evidently no thought of surrender. The fire, although hot, was ill-directed, and comparatively little damage was done. Nevertheless Moray, though he still mastered himself with mighty efforts of self-control, winced as if he had been hit himself, when any of the blue-jackets or marines were wounded. They might have escaped had the corvette used her guns, and so it seemed to him that he was personally responsible for each of those casualties. He only longed to be at close quarters with the enemy; but, in the meantime, his attention and theirs was diverted. To his astonishment and disgust, he saw Leslie, who the moment before had been standing by his side, crouching under the gunwale of the launch, out of the way of danger. The sympathy of the rough seamen had suddenly changed to contempt; and now, indifferent to the bullets that came thicker and flew straighter, they were passing their rough jokes on the land-lubber whose nerves had fairly got the better of him.

At the sight of his nephew's cowardice, Moray almost forgot his daughter's danger. He sprang forward to lay a hand on Leslie's shoulder, and shook him savagely.

" By the God who made us ! I would rather know Grace was dead, than give her to a man who shows the white feather at——"

He stopped short before the sentence was finished. He scarcely knew his nephew's face, distorted as it was by the intensity of suppressed passion. No Malay among those who kept his daughter a prisoner could have worn an expression of more determined ferocity. The gentle-mannered poet seemed transformed, as, turning round sharply and fiercely, he saw who had touched him, and said in hasty explanation—

" One of those stray bullets might hit me, and rob me of the chance of rescue or revenge."

And as Moray, excited and preoccupied as he was, shrank back at the unexpected display of passion—Jack Venables, remembering what had passed at the interview in London, might have been less surprised—he recognised the depth of the affection that was ready to die under an indelible stain, rather than play the *rôle* of a looker-on in the hand-to-hand struggle that was approaching.

There was little time for Leslie's limbs to get cramped in the undignified position to which he had resigned himself. The Malay war-shouts were answered with ringing cheers; the last volley from the enemy's firearms was followed by some groans and a death-cry; and in another moment the boats were grappling themselves to the prahus. Then seamen and marines, who had reserved their fire, poured in point-blank volleys with deadly effect, and under cover of the confusion they were swarming up the sides, with cutlasses and bayonets flashing in the sunbeams. The lustre of the English weapons was speedily dimmed, for the Malays fought gallantly and desperately. But their irregular ferocity was in vain against the British dash and the British discipline. The fight was bloody, but it was soon over; the prahus that had been directly attacked were carried, the defenders being either cut down at their posts or throwing themselves into the water and striking out for the others. And when the flag of the pirate chief was hauled down, and his galley was seen to be in the hands of the white men, there was a general *sauve qui peut* from the rest of the fleet. Brave as the Malays were, they bowed to the force of circumstances; and they had a wholesome terror of the guns of the big ship, which had not as yet been brought into action. As they could not save their boats, they tried to save themselves; and the glowing surface of the sea was sparkling in a driving spray of diamonds, where innumerable heads and shoulders were seen striking out for the shore.

The struggle had been brief, and no Englishman hung back in it; but Leslie had been to the front in it from the first, among scores of other brave men.

"For heaven's sake, don't be so foolhardy, Mr Leslie!" the first lieutenant had found time to shout in an ear that was absolutely deaf to the well-meant expostulation.

"Hech, sir, div ye see hoo the deevil fechts!" ejaculated a countryman of his own, complacently, as he paused to breathe himself, and to wipe his brow, between the mighty strokes he was laying on the Malays.

Indifferent alike to praise and prudence, Leslie flung himself into the foremost of the *mêlée*, forcing his way towards the barbarian who seemed to be the leader. The barbaric warrior was a powerful man, who might have made one and a half of Miss Moray's lover. He honoured his assailant with a downright sword-cut, that should have " cleft him to the chine," to borrow the language of the chroniclers of the middle age, had not a sailor seasonably interposed a cutlass, when the blow glanced, merely bruising a shoulder, and ere the Malay could recover his weapon, the poet had run him through the body. How little he thought, when he had been " mooning " and dreaming at Glenconan, that he would ever have so dramatic an opportunity of proving his devotion to his lady !

But was the lady safe ? that was the next question ; and a question neither the father nor the lover almost dared to ask. The Malays cut down, driven overboard, or secured, the next business was to search the boat—no very difficult matter. There was only one possible place of concealment in the half-decked craft ; but the hatches were strong, and lashed down with bamboo cordage. There was a call for cutlasses to sever the cords, and the very embarrassment of eager volunteers delayed the business. As we cannot depict the spasm of agonising expectation, as father and lover burst from the sunshine into the blackness of the little cabin, so we must drop a veil over the scene that followed, when the seamen, delicately surging back, dropped a mat over the family reunion. Grace was there, and Grace was safe; quit from the horrors and the fears and hopes of her last twenty-four hours' experiences.

"Her pluck does her some credit, does it not?" said Moray proudly, when he presented her to Captain MacDonald above the gangway of the Severn, as pale as she seemed calm, but none the less pretty for her pallor. "Not that there is much to choose between the two in that respect," as he turned round beamingly towards Leslie, who followed them. "Lucky dog!" was the gallant captain's inward comment, as he received Miss Moray's effusions of heart-felt gratitude, only regretting that this prize of love had been already appropriated by its salvor. And "lucky dog!"

was the sentiment that in various language was re-echoed by the ship's company, from the wardroom officers to the powder-monkeys; and so closed that episode of nautical romance, which will long be spun in yarns round the Severn's galley-fires.

CHAPTER XLII.

MARRIED IN HASTE.

THE telegrams requesting the despatch of the Severn to Sanga had thrown Mr Venables into extreme perturbation and excitement. That bit of business off his hands, he was doomed to the suspense he detested. Communications between Sanga and the Straits were so precarious, that he might hear nothing more for any number of weeks. Meantime his friends might be massacred, and he could do nothing to help them. That last reflection was so much to the point, that it might have reconciled a less impulsive young gentleman to resignation and the exercise of patience. But to the warm-hearted Jack such inaction was out of the question; he felt that it was incumbent upon him to be up and doing. So, silencing the whispers of hard common-sense, and having made up his mind on the subject, he thought it would be a satisfaction to consult some one. Acknowledging his weakness, he did not care to turn either to Lord Wrekin or to one of the Government Whips, or even to his stanch friend and patron, Lord Wrekin's brother. Of all people in the world, he chose Miss Winstanley for his adviser; though, indeed, they had been in the habit lately of laying their heads together on most occasions.

Julia heard all he had to say; but it struck him she was somewhat less sympathetic than usual. She objected very sensibly that he could do no possible good, as he must reach Sanga long after everything had been settled. As Jack could only plead sentiment for his plan, he was less persuasive than usual; but we may suspect that Miss Winstanley attributed his embarrassment to a different cause.

"You see, Leslie saved my life," he wound up. "I vowed and felt undying gratitude, and I can't bear to think of his possibly perishing, without my stirring a finger to help him."

"It seems to me you already discharged great part of the debt, when you so generously resigned the girl you were both in love with," said Miss Winstanley, drily. "Besides," she repeated very pertinently, "though you well know how grieved I should be were anything to happen either to Grace or Mr Leslie, you must feel that your going to Sumatra would be worse than idle in the circumstances."

"I fear that is true; still going would be a relief to my mind, and I should always feel that at least I had acknowledged my debt, which is the next best thing to being able to discharge it. And after all, the Severn may have been in time to save them; and think what a pleasure it would be to be there to congratulate them on their escape. Though, if Leslie got out in time for any fighting, if he has not fallen in the engagement it will be no fault of his. You may take my word for that, Julia."

"My name is Miss Winstanley, *Mr* Venables, and no doubt it *would* be a pleasure to console your cousin."

Hardly had the words been spoken, than Julia was heartily ashamed of them, and she saw, besides, to her infinite confusion, that she had betrayed herself. Jack looked at her steadily, till her eyes sank beneath his gaze; then he spoke very deliberately, but with more diffidence than was usual with him.

"I might remind you, *Miss* Winstanley," and he laid an ironical emphasis on her name, "that it was you who confirmed me in my good resolution of giving up my cousin when I could not help it. The sacrifice was all the easier, that I knew in my heart she had never cared for me, — never cared for me, that is to say, as she cared for Ralph Leslie. And knowing that, though I shall never lose my affection for her, I was long ago as effectively cured of my passion as any man need desire to be."

Jack watched the effect of his speech, and saw the lady brightening through her blushes, which turned suspicion into something like assurance. "Shall I say something more, now I am in course of confession? Shall I tell you how another idol made that fancy fade?"

Jack was very near saying something of

those signs of jealousy he had detected, but he discreetly checked himself. Then, as Julia's silence carried conviction to his mind, he recovered all his natural audacity, and, like the Malays charging home upon Sanga, he went at the feeble defences with a rush.

"What is the use of beating about the bushes? You are far too quick not to have understood my feelings long ago. I love Grace Moray as a cousin; but I would adore you as a wife, if you will only say the word, and give me the permission. Why did I come to you now, in place of going to consult with your father, but because I would have you the mistress of my actions, as you have long been the object of my thoughts — Julia!"

Still the young lady said nothing; but this time she did not object to the use of her Christian name. So Jack stole an arm round her waist, and drew her to his side, softly unresisting. In his anxiety for the answer, no doubt, he laid his cheek to hers. The answer, when it did come, seemed quite satisfactory, though it was merely, "And yet you mean to leave me?"

"Not a bit of it," exclaimed Jack, in an exuberance of spirits, seizing her in his arms, and cutting short any further speech by a short and summary process. "Not a bit of it," he went on, when he had time to take breath. "You know I pride myself on my inspirations, and I have a happy inspiration now."

"And what may that be?" asked Julia, blushingly rearranging her hair.

"Simply that we should get married to-morrow or next day, have our honeymoon on board the steamer, and make our wedding-trip to Sumatra."

"What nonsense!" exclaimed Julia, very naturally. She seemed now to take the necessary preliminaries to a wedding-trip for granted, and the marriage as merely a question of time.

"Nonsense, dearest! not at all," exclaimed Jack, briskly. Then he went on more seriously, "I *must* start for Sumatra at once : my feelings are not to be reasoned with; and I am sure you will not attempt it. I know that my—I mean our—future peace depends on it. But you like the Morays nearly as much as I

do, and why in the world should we not go
and see after them together? I shall look on
our marriage as such a blessed omen, that I
begin to believe already we shall find them all
safe and sound. And what a place for our
honeymooning the Spice Islands will be!
While, if the worst should have happened, I
shall have you by my side: and Heaven only
knows how I should need your companionship
in that case."

"That might be a reason," sighed Julia,
softly. "If it were anyways possible," she
added, as a saving clause.

But when Jack and Julia did lay their
heads together, metaphorically and literally,
they were just the pair to overcome apparent
impossibilities. Mr Winstanley, though somewhat surprised, was far from objecting to the
match; and on second thoughts he rather
fancied the idea of carrying it through speedily and unconventionally. It is to be feared
that his wife's first indignant protests rather
helped to overrule his hesitation; and Julia
found means of managing her mother. Possibly Mrs Winstanley may have thought—
although there she wronged her daughter—

that the young lady might have been persuaded to elope, and she may have deemed
that a sensation was preferable to a scandal.
And if an immediate wedding were once decided upon, as Julia pointed out, it must
necessarily be of the quietest, seeing that the
fate of so many of " dear Jack's " near relatives
was something more than uncertain. At all
events, it is a fact, and an incontestable proof
of the energy of Jack's character, though it
may seem to violate the credibilities of ortho-
dox fiction, that within a week the settlements
were signed, and Mr Venables and his bride
were before the altar. The father of the
bridegroom, with efficient "assistance," tied
the knot ; a couple of the bridegroom's sisters,
and as many of the bride's cousins, officiated as
bridesmaids ; and though the wedding-break-
fast was a quiet and rather melancholy meal,
all things were done decently and in order.

"You are a very fortunate man, Mr Jack,
though it is I who tell you so," said Winstanley. "Had any one said that Julia would
sacrifice a trousseau, and consent to be smug-
gled away in a hole - and - corner ceremony,
I should have set him down for a lunatic

Believe an old man of the world, that my girl must be passionately in love with you, and the fault will be yours if she does not make you happy."

And, *apropos* to happiness, the bride had had a happy thought of her own, when the bridegroom was bustling through the innumerable preparations.

"I have been thinking, dear, of a man we might take out with us to Sanga."

"Well, as you please, darling," said Jack, doubtfully. "I don't think any fellow we could engage would be much use to us. We can always pick up a native in the East—a salamander, who would be suitable to the climate."

"I was thinking of a Scotchman, not a salamander."

"My dear Julia!"—and there was already a touch of marital authority in the ejaculation, though Jack did gulp down the "are you mad?" which was to follow.

The intonation did not escape the sensitive ears of the lady; but she only smiled, and said, "Donald Ross."

"The very thing!" exclaimed Jack, enthusiastically. "By Jove, Julia! what a head —what a heart you have! I suppose you can manage to square things with his master; so I shall despatch a telegram this very moment, and we can send Mr Ross his marching orders by the evening's post. My word for it, he will lose no time in getting ready."

CHAPTER XLIII.

MARRIED AT LEISURE.

THE Severn, after a week passed at Sanga, had steamed back to Penang. For a week the managing director had entertained the saviour of his daughter with all the hospitality of which the circumstances admitted. It was little that the Residency had been sacked and wrecked; they picnicked pleasantly enough in the open. There were sad casualties to deplore, though chiefly among the natives; but the dead had been burned with their dwellings or buried out of sight. The gallant captain of the Severn found himself so comfortable, that had things been different he might have extended his stay. But he was sincerely smitten with Miss Moray, who, although really grateful, seemed to have only eyes and ears for Mr

Leslie; so that Captain MacDonald deemed
it wise to remember the duty he owed to his
admiral. And thus it came about that in a
reasonably short space of time telegraphic
information was transmitted from the Straits
of the onslaught on the Settlement and the
punishment of the assailants. And when the
newly wedded pair arrived at Port Said, they
found news awaiting them which set their
minds at ease. Thenceforth the voyage was
to be really a pleasure-trip, and they might
give themselves over to *rattraper* any time
they had lost in the way of billing and
cooing. Thenceforward Donald Ross brightened up from the gloom that had made him
almost a misanthrope; and not only was he
always ready to have "a crack" about the
Highlands with Mr and Mrs Venables, or any
of the cabin passengers, but he contributed
greatly to the cheerfulness of the ship's company forward. As for Jack, he was more and
more delighted with Julia in her new characters of wife and constant companion, and
congratulated himself hourly on his greatest
stroke of good luck. As for Julia, she had
been softened by the sweetening influences

of the honeymoon, and hung upon her husband with shy caresses in a spring bloom of
new-born graces; and as the days glided by
upon silken wings, they were both looking
forward with growing delight to the surprise
they were preparing for their friends in
Sanga.

"Grace will give me a warmer welcome
than on that memorable visit of mine to
Glenconan," said Julia; "all the more so
that I have effectually relieved her of those
most unwelcome attentions of yours, sir."

"Leslie will know, at least," said Jack,
disdainfully ignoring the insulting allusion,
"that if I did not turn up in the hour of
their extremity, it was the power and not the
will that was wanting. And in thinking of
their lives being safe, we have almost forgotten the salvage of their fortunes. Yet but
a few months ago, how glad my uncle would
have been to know that he might keep
Glenconan, though at the cost of the rest
of his fortune! Our budget of good news
will be the best of wedding-gifts for that
other marriage which ought to come off
immediately."

And on their arrival at Penang, Jack's proverbial good luck still befriended them; for they would have felt the annoyances of an indefinite' delay almost as deeply as Leslie had done. A commodious enough trader, bound for Sarambang, was easily persuaded to diverge by Sanga; and fruits and other sea luxuries were shipped in profusion, that the sail might be made as agreeable as possible to the bride.

Had the colonists needed occupation in the transports of their reunion and recovered happiness, they had plenty of it in the meantime at Sanga. The Residency was to be reconstructed — an easy matter, where bamboos were as abundant as native labour. Beggared families had to be relieved; widows were to be consoled and orphans to be cared for; and in these good works we need hardly say that Grace and her lover went hand in hand with the Resident. Matusin had come back, having saved himself narrowly after a stubborn resistance; and had been duly praised for his gallantry by his chief, with promises of rewards and advancement. Rafferty had recovered, of course, and seemed little the worse for that broken head of his, which came so naturally to the Tipperary man. And Mr Briggs had been rescued with Grace, having been knocked over at his post beside the fire-proof safe, and carried bound hand and foot on board the piratical prahu. It was the respectable Briggs, above all, whom the Resident seemed most to delight to honour, though perhaps he felt a warmer personal regard for Mr Rafferty, who had so devotedly attached himself to the fortunes of his daughter. But in the case of Briggs, he could appreciate the heroism, where a clerk-like and conscientious sense of duty had triumphed over the feeble flesh.

So, on the whole, that population of many shades formed a happy and contented family: for semi-savages get over calamities and even bereavements, as severe flesh-wounds heal quickly with the wild creatures of the jungles. Especially as when in the present instance there was a liberal application of plasters in the shape of kindness and cash.

Yet, happily contented as they were, a sensation is a sensation; and there was general excitement when, one day at dawn, a European trader in the offing was seen signalling for a boat and a pilot.

"Had it been a fortnight later," said Moray, "it might have been our new furniture from Penang : as it is, that is altogether out of the question. If it were not that dignity forbids, and that I have an appointment with Matusin moreover, I would go down and see the skipper disembark."

"Dignity does not forbid me," said Leslie, "nor you either, for that matter, Miss Resident : it won't be very hot for an hour or two ; suppose you order your palanquin."

Grace was only too willing. She would follow Leslie nowadays as Finette followed her.

The palanquin was halted beneath a clump of cocoa-palms ; Grace got out, and, guided by her cousin, sought shade still further out of the sun, where for a few minutes, as was very much the fashion with them, they forgot about the visitors and all the world besides. It was the sound of voices, borne through the still air, that roused them. A boat was pulling swiftly towards the shore : the ship was still lying off in the bay. Leslie negligently

unslung a pair of race-glasses, and focussed
them on the boat. All at once he uttered a
tremendous ejaculation, and thrust the glasses
into his companion's hands. "Look there,
Grace!—and then tell me if we are waking
or dreaming."

Grace looked, and gave a low cry of delight,
as if she doubted the evidence of her senses,
and yet was unwilling to awaken and be un-
deceived. And Finette, roused from her slumber, came whimpering to her mistress's side.

"Well, what do you make of him?" asked
her lover, smiling.

"It cannot; and yet it must be. And if
old Donald is in that boat off Sumatra, who
can the people be on board that ship?"

"Jack Venables for one," answered Leslie,
confidently.

But Grace now had only eyes for the boat.
After all, as Leslie was delighted to remember,
all she held most dear was with her in Sanga.
And what she saw was an apparition unpre-
cedented in these seas : the stalwart figure of
her dear old friend, in complete Celtic costume. Hardly, perhaps, could Donald have
given a greater proof of his affection, than in

defying the climate and its plagues, that his young mistress might be reminded of Glenconan. The broad Highland bonnet invited sun-stroke, as the unguarded legs were irresistibly tempting to the venomous swarms of mosquitoes and sand-flies. Donald, in spite of his overstrung feelings, slapped and suffered and swore; but his tormentors and sufferings were all forgotten, when he saw " Miss Grace " rushing down with outstretched hands to welcome him. He almost fell and fawned at his lady's feet, as Finette, with her joyful whines, was leaping up and licking his face.

It was a merry dinner that night at the Residency; none the less so, perhaps, that there was an under-current of deep and earnest feeling. By way of fillip to its conviviality, Jack had communicated the good news of the unexpectedly favourable prospects of the bank liquidation. According to all appearances, the assets Campbell had placed at the disposal of the liquidators had so far lightened the obligations of the shareholders that there was no probability of further calls. It was possible, on the contrary, that there might be a return of moneys. In any case, if Moray's investments were swept away, he might leave an unencumbered estate to his daughter. The most sensitive conscience might consider any early indiscretions as purged, and hencefor-ward he was a free, and should be a happy, man.

It was a merry dinner, but a merrier cere-mony was soon to follow. Mrs Venables had declared that, much as she was enchanted with Sanga, it was indispensable that they should cut their visit short. And even the hospitable Moray had little to say when she gave him her reasons for the decision.

" Jack would start at a moment's notice, and I was foolish enough to consent to come with him. But he has left everything at sixes and sevens: his chief in the lurch—irritated constituents—not that that greatly signifies in the circumstances,—and speculations in the charge of my father, whose ignorance of them aggravates his responsibilities. No, my dear Mr Moray, we must go back very soon ; other-wise I should always blame myself for any misfortunes that might happen."

Moray had nothing to object, and could only consent rather ruefully.

"But, before we go, I have a favour to ask, and I fancy you know what I mean."

"*Demande toujours.*"

"As we have come so far for so little, seeing we have found you all safe, we should wish to have the wedding happily over."

"The story of the fox who lost his own tail, Mrs Venables; and so I suppose it was in malice prepense you gave the chaplain of the Settlement a passage from Penang. Well, what will be will be; and, for my own part, I see no reason for delay. You had best speak to Leslie on the subject, and I don't doubt you will find him amenable."

Leslie so literally jumped at the suggestion, that he scarcely restrained his expressions of delight at the approaching departure of the visitors, as Mrs Venables resentfully remarked; while Grace was too fondly proud to care to play the coquette; and if less demonstrative than Ralph, she was to the full as compliant. Though to him indeed she was outspoken enough, and placed herself as generously at his disposal as any lover need have desired.

"As you will have me, Ralph, you may take me when you will; you have won the right to command me a thousand times over."

And Ralph could have fallen down and wor-shipped ; only he compromised by clasping her in his embrace,—a " passage of arms " which had come so naturally to him of late, that there was nothing very novel in it to either.

CHAPTER XLIV.

L'ENVOI.

To Leslie the circumstances of his wedding seemed the very irony of destiny. A quiet fellow naturally, of dreamy temperament and unobtrusive disposition, he would have liked to have taken Grace in a village church, with her father to give her away, and the clerk and a pew-duster for witnesses. And here he was to be one of the central figures in a sort of international ceremony, where, in the pomp of oriental display, a subject people were to make holiday.

"You might have been much worse off, old fellow," remarked Jack, consolingly. "You might have been married at St George's, with a bishop to officiate, and a dozen of bridesmaids before a trooping of the fashions."

"Thank you for reminding me of that,"

answered Leslie, gratefully. "Trust you for
always looking at things on their sunny side.
Not that there is likely to be any lack of sunshine; and seven in the morning for a
marriage seems to be rather an uncanonical
hour."

Considering the noise that was made in the
Settlement, he might have been married much
earlier, for all the sleep he got. The loyal subjects of the Sumatra Company had been wide-
awake all night like the mosquitoes, blazing
away blank charges from rusty firearms, and
letting off all manner of native squibs and
crackers. No one would have guessed that,
only a few weeks before, the Settlement had
been sacked by pirates. It seemed good policy
to encourage the people in their rejoicings on
so very exceptional an occasion; so Moray had
been liberal of largesses, and had served out
powder freely. And the Malays of the lower
orders had plenty to look at, besides the unfamiliar spectacle of a Christian wedding, and
the still less familiar sight of a beautiful and
unveiled bride. The chiefs of the country,
from the Sultan downwards, delighted to worship the rising sun and the power of the

victorious English. The Sultan could hardly condescend so far as to attend the ceremony in person ; but our old acquaintance, Pangaran Jaffir, brought presents in his name,—strings of orient pearls, and massive bracelets of gold and emerald. Many a minor chief came with his train of followers, whom Moray received with the rough old Highland hospitality, finding them free quarters *al fresco*, with any quantity of food and drink by way of bedding and night-clothes. And there was Matusin, at the head of his household and the notables of Sanga, proud of the slash across his cheek, received from one of the piratical *krises*. There, among the Malays, was Donald Ross, in his tartans, dwarfing most of them by his height, broad shoulders and muscle, and looking as warlike as any. And by Donald's side was the facetious Mr Rafferty, with whom the Highlander had sworn eternal brotherhood, since he learned how the Irishman had stood by Miss Grace. By the way, when everybody, whether with a claim or without one, was asking favours, Mr Rafferty had prepared a petition to Miss Moray.

"By all means, Rafferty," she had said, " I

think I may promise before you ask. I am certain you will ask nothing unreasonable."

"Unraisonable! and sure, thin, it is the most raisonable thing in life; for it's sad you would be were your wedding to be a sorrow to me."

"Well, then, Rafferty, tell me what I can do for you."

"Just this, Miss. Divil the drop of drink has passed my lips since the night thim vagabonds broke into the Risidincy. I don't rightly remimber how long I took the pledge for: and 'deed maybe it was the better for me, with my broken head. But I would like to be at liberty to get drunk to-morrow, were it to happen so, with an aisy conscience; and it would only be civil to Mr Ross if I were ready to take a drop with him."

Grace laughed, though she felt the request and the consequent responsibility to be embarrassing.

"Take the drop with Donald, by all means, Rafferty; and as for the rest, I leave it to you. I am sure that, on that day of all others, you would not wish to make me ashamed of one of the best of my friends."

Whereupon Rafferty had scratched his head and thanked her, though only half satisfied. He was bound to keep sober now, under any circumstances; and it seemed to him that it was dishonouring so solemn an occasion. " But, after all," so he consoled himself, " it was herself that bid me do it; and Heaven knows it will be by no wish of my own if I should be as well - behaved as any of thim water-drinking niggers."

So Mr Rafferty kept himself strictly sober; but otherwise the ceremony went off very well. Mr Venables proposed the health of the newly married couple in a neat and appropriate speech, and Leslie acknowledged all he owed to his friend in more effusive and touching language than he dared have used had the *déjeuner* come off in a London dining-room. As for the bride, her eyes had filled with tears, and yet Mrs Venables was so far from feeling jealous that she shared Mrs Leslie's emotion. Perhaps the feature of the proceedings was the Resident's speech, in which he lauded to the skies both Briggs and Rafferty. Briggs broke down, as was only natural, in an almost inarticulate attempt at acknowledgment; and even the Irishman, for once, was covered with confusion, and rejoiced that his humble position sealed his lips. He contented himself with dealing Donald Ross, who was sitting next to him and cheering vociferously, a friendly blow in the ribs with his elbow.

Old shoes were scarce in the Settlement, since the population wore sandals; but we need not say that, having regard to the latitude and the produce of the country, there was no lack of rice to send in showers after the pair when they embarked in a boat for the improvised bungalow in a clearing, where they were to pass the first days of the honeymoon. Heavenly as was the climate, romantic as were the surroundings, and delightfully as the lovers were wrapped up in each other, they would not have been sorry to have returned from savagery to civilisation, and to have exchanged the volcanic craters of the Sanga chain for the cloud-capped summits of Glenconan. Julia had taken it for granted that if Grace did not accompany her home—and, to tell the truth, she could quite understand that each might prefer to have her husband to herself in the meantime—nevertheless she was sure to follow very speedily. But to that apparently natural arrangement an insurmountable obstacle was interposed. Moray, although again the unembarrassed master of his inheritance, and still sufficiently rich — although far less wealthy than he had been—declined altogether to resign his post. "I may die at Glenconan, and I trust I shall; but God has given me a duty to discharge here in the meantime. I have life enough left, I believe, to settle 'the Settlement'; nor do I intend to turn my back on the task till it is accomplished. It was in the East I erred, and in the East I have the opportunity of atoning, at all events, for early errors."

From that firm decision there was no driving him ; and his daughter and his son-in-law knew him too well to attempt doing so. But being infinitely happy in each other where they were, it was no great sacrifice to prolong their exile ; and Moray, being willing to concede something on 'his side, had the grace to acquiesce in the sacrifice. " Everything comes to those who wait," he remarked to Mr Venables; "and when the nursery has to be furnished, they must furnish the nursery at Glenconan !"

As for Donald Ross, we need hardly say that he decided on prolonging his leave of absence indefinitely, sending Mr Winstanley his dutiful respects and his demission as head-keeper. Though in sticking to "Miss Grace" and the fortunes of his former master, like his master he by no means gave up the expectation of being gathered to his fathers in his native glen.

THE END.

PRINTED BY WILLIAM BLACKWOOD AND SONS.

CATALOGUE

OF

MESSRS BLACKWOOD & SONS'

PUBLICATIONS.

PHILOSOPHICAL CLASSICS FOR ENGLISH READERS.

EDITED BY WILLIAM KNIGHT, LL.D.,

Professor of Moral Philosophy in the University of St Andrews.

In crown 8vo Volumes, with Portraits, price 3s. 6d.

Now ready—

1. **Descartes.** By Professor MAHAFFY, Dublin.
2. **Butler.** By Rev. W. LUCAS COLLINS, M.A.
3. **Berkeley.** By Professor FRASER, Edinburgh.
4. **Fichte.** By Professor ADAMSON, Owens College, Manchester.
5. **Kant.** By Professor WALLACE, Oxford.
6. **Hamilton.** By Professor VEITCH, Glasgow.
7. **Hegel.** By Professor EDWARD CAIRD, Glasgow.
8. **Leibniz.** By J. THEODORE MERZ.
9. **Vico.** By Professor FLINT, Edinburgh.
10. **Hobbes.** By Professor CROOM ROBERTSON, London.

The Volumes in preparation are—

HUME. By the Editor. | SPINOZA. By the Very Rev. Principal
BACON. By Professor Nichol, Glasgow. | Caird, Glasgow.

IN COURSE OF PUBLICATION.

FOREIGN CLASSICS FOR ENGLISH READERS.

EDITED BY MRS OLIPHANT.

In Crown 8vo, 2s. 6d.

The Volumes published are—

DANTE. By the Editor.
VOLTAIRE. By Major-General Sir E. B. Hamley, K.C.M.G.
PASCAL. By Principal Tulloch.
PETRARCH. By Henry Reeve, C.B.
GOETHE. By A. Hayward, Q.C.
MOLIÈRE. By the Editor and F. Tarver, M.A.
MONTAIGNE. By Rev. W. L. Collins, M.A.
RABELAIS. By Walter Besant, M.A.
CALDERON. By E. J. Hasell.

SAINT SIMON. By Clifton W. Collins, M.A.
CERVANTES. By the Editor.
CORNEILLE AND RACINE. By Henry M. Trollope.
MADAME DE SÉVIGNÉ. By Miss Thackeray.
LA FONTAINE, AND OTHER FRENCH FABULISTS. By Rev. W. Lucas Collins, M.A.
SCHILLER. By James Sime, M.A., Author of 'Lessing: his Life and Writings.'
TASSO. By E. J. Hasell.
ROUSSEAU. By Henry Grey Graham.

*In preparation—*LEOPARDI, by the Editor.

NOW COMPLETE.

ANCIENT CLASSICS FOR ENGLISH READERS.

EDITED BY THE REV. W. LUCAS COLLINS, M.A.

Complete in 28 Vols. crown 8vo, cloth, price 2s. 6d. each. And may also be had in 14 Volumes, strongly and neatly bound, with calf or vellum back, £3, 10s.

Saturday Review.—"It is difficult to estimate too highly the value of such a series as this in giving 'English readers' an insight, exact as far as it goes, into those olden times which are so remote and yet to many of us so close."

CATALOGUE

OF

MESSRS BLACKWOOD & SONS'

PUBLICATIONS.

ALISON. History of Europe. By Sir ARCHIBALD ALISON, Bart., D.C.L.

1. From the Commencement of the French Revolution to the Battle of Waterloo.
   LIBRARY EDITION, 14 vols., with Portraits. Demy 8vo, £10, 10s.
   ANOTHER EDITION, in 20 vols. crown 8vo, £6.
   PEOPLE'S EDITION, 13 vols. crown 8vo, £2, 11s.

2. Continuation to the Accession of Louis Napoleon.
   LIBRARY EDITION, 8 vols. 8vo, £6, 7s. 6d.
   PEOPLE'S EDITION, 8 vols. crown 8vo, 34s.

3. Epitome of Alison's History of Europe. Twenty-ninth Thousand, 7s. 6d.

4. Atlas to Alison's History of Europe. By A. Keith Johnston.
   LIBRARY EDITION, demy 4to, £3, 3s.
   PEOPLE'S EDITION, 31s. 6d.

—— Life of John Duke of Marlborough. With some Account of his Contemporaries, and of the War of the Succession. Third Edition, 2 vols. 8vo. Portraits and Maps, 30s.

—— Essays: Historical, Political, and Miscellaneous. 3 vols. demy 8vo, 45s.

—— Lives of Lord Castlereagh and Sir Charles Stewart, Second and Third Marquesses of Londonderry. From the Original Papers of the Family. 3 vols. 8vo, £2, 2s.

ADAMS. Great Campaigns. A Succinct Account of the Principal Military Operations which have taken place in Europe from 1796 to 1870. By Major C. ADAMS, Professor of Military History at the Staff College. Edited by Captain C. COOPER KING, R.M. Artillery, Instructor of Tacti Royal Military College. 8vo, with Maps. 16s.

AIRD. Poetical Works of Thomas Aird. Fifth Edition, with Memoir of the Author by the Rev. JARDINE WALLACE, and Portrait. Crown 8vo, 7s. 6d.

ALLARDYCE. The City of Sunshine. By ALEXANDER ALLARDYCE. Three vols. post 8vo, £1, 5s. 6d.

—— Memoir of the Honourable George Keith Elphinstone, K.B., Viscount Keith of Stonehaven Marischal, Admiral of the Red. One vol. 8vo, with Portrait, Illustrations, and Maps. 21s.

BRACKENBURY. The River Column : A Narrative of the Advance of the River Column of the Nile Expeditionary Force, and its Return down the Rapids. By Major-General HENRY BRACKENBURY, C.B., Late Commanding the River Column With Maps by Major the Hon. F. L. L. COLBORNE, Royal Irish Rifles. Crown 8vo, 7s. 6d.

BROADLEY. Tunis, Past and Present. With a Narrative of the French Conquest of the Regency. By A. M. BROADLEY. With numerous Illustrations and Maps. 2 vols. post 8vo. 25s.

BROOKE, Life of Sir James, Rajah of Sarāwak. From his Personal Papers and Correspondence. By SPENSER ST JOHN, H.M.'s Minister-Resident and Consul-General Peruvian Republic ; formerly Secretary to the Rajah. With Portrait and a Map. Post 8vo, 12s. 6d.

BROUGHAM. Memoirs of the Life and Times of Henry Lord Brougham. Written by HIMSELF. 3 vols. 8vo, £2, 8s. The Volumes are sold separately, price 16s. each.

BROWN. The Forester : A Practical Treatise on the Planting, Rearing, and General Management of Forest-trees. By JAMES BROWN, LL.D., Inspector of and Reporter on Woods and Forests, Benmore House, Port Elgin, Ontario. Fifth Edition, revised and enlarged. Royal 8vo, with Engravings. 36s.

BROWN. The Ethics of George Eliot's Works. By JOHN CROMBIE BROWN. Fourth Edition. Crown 8vo, 2s. 6d.

BROWN. A Manual of Botany, Anatomical and Physiological. For the Use of Students. By ROBERT BROWN, M.A., Ph.D. Crown 8vo, with numerous Illustrations, 12s. 6d.

BUCHAN. Introductory Text-Book of Meteorology. By ALEXANDER BUCHAN, M.A., F.R.S.E., Secretary of the Scottish Meteorological Society, &c. Crown 8vo, with 8 Coloured Charts and other Engravings, pp. 218. 4s. 6d.

BUCHANAN. The Shire Highlands (East Central Africa). By JOHN BUCHANAN, Planter at Zomba. Crown 8vo, 5s.

BURBIDGE. Domestic Floriculture, Window Gardening, and Floral Decorations. Being practical directions for the Propagation, Culture, and Arrangement of Plants and Flowers as Domestic Ornaments. By F. W. BURBIDGE. Second Edition. Crown 8vo, with numerous Illustrations, 7s. 6d.

———— Cultivated Plants : Their Propagation and Improvement. Including Natural and Artificial Hybridisation, Raising from Seed, Cuttings, and Layers, Grafting and Budding, as applied to the Families and Genera in Cultivation. Crown 8vo, with numerous Illustrations, 12s. 6d.

BURTON. The History of Scotland : From Agricola's Invasion to the Extinction of the last Jacobite Insurrection. By JOHN HILL BURTON, D.C.L., Historiographer-Royal for Scotland. New and Enlarged Edition, 8 vols., and Index. Crown 8vo, £3, 3s.

———— History of the British Empire during the Reign of Queen Anne. In 3 vols. 8vo. 36s.

———— The Scot Abroad. New Edition. Crown 8vo, 10s. 6d.

———— The Book-Hunter. New Edition. Crown 8vo, 7s. 6d.

BUTE. The Roman Breviary : Reformed by Order of the Holy Œcumenical Council of Trent ; Published by Order of Pope St Pius V.; and Revised by Clement VIII. and Urban VIII.; together with the Offices since granted. Translated out of Latin into English by JOHN, Marquess of Bute, K.T. In 2 vols. crown 8vo, cloth boards, edges uncut. £2, 2s.

———— The Altus of St Columba. With a Prose Paraphrase and Notes. In paper cover, 2s. 6d.

BUTT. Miss Molly. By BEATRICE MAY BUTT. Cheap Edition, 2s.

———— Geraldine Hawthorne : A Sketch. By the Author of 'Miss Molly.' Crown 8vo, 7s. 6d.

BUTT. Alison. By the Author of 'Miss Molly.' 3 vols. crown 8vo, 25s. 6d.

CAIRD. Sermons. By JOHN CAIRD, D.D., Principal of the University of Glasgow. Sixteenth Thousand. Fcap. 8vo, 5s.

———— Religion in Common Life. A Sermon preached in Crathie Church, October 14, 1855, before Her Majesty the Queen and Prince Albert. Published by Her Majesty's Command. Cheap Edition, 3d.

CAMERON. Gaelic Names of Plants (Scottish and Irish). Collected and Arranged in Scientific Order, with Notes on their Etymology, their Uses, Plant Superstitions, &c., among the Celts, with copious Gaelic, English, and Scientific Indices. By JOHN CAMERON, Sunderland. 8vo, 7s. 6d.

CAMPBELL. Sermons Preached before the Queen at Balmoral. By the Rev. A. A. CAMPBELL, Minister of Crathie. Published by Command of Her Majesty. Crown 8vo, 4s. 6d.

CAMPBELL. Records of Argyll. Legends, Traditions, and Recollections of Argyllshire Highlanders, collected chiefly from the Gaelic. With Notes on the Antiquity of the Dress, Clan Colours or Tartans of the Highlanders. By LORD ARCHIBALD CAMPBELL. Illustrated with Nineteen full-page Etchings. 4to, printed on hand-made paper, £3, 3s.

CAPPON. Victor Hugo. A Memoir and a Study. By JAMES CAPPON, M.A. Post 8vo, 10s. 6d.

CARRICK. Koumiss; or, Fermented Mare's Milk: and its Uses in the Treatment and Cure of Pulmonary Consumption, and other Wasting Diseases. With an Appendix on the best Methods of Fermenting Cow's Milk. By GEORGE L. CARRICK, M.D., L.R.C.S.E. and L.R.C.P.E., Physician to the British Embassy, St Petersburg, &c. Crown 8vo, 10s. 6d.

CAUVIN. A Treasury of the English and German Languages. Compiled from the best Authors and Lexicographers in both Languages. Adapted to the Use of Schools, Students, Travellers, and Men of Business; and forming a Companion to all German-English Dictionaries. By JOSEPH CAUVIN, LL.D. & Ph.D., of the University of Göttingen, &c. Crown 8vo, 7s. 6d.

CAVE-BROWN. Lambeth Palace and its Associations. By J. CAVE-BROWN, M.A., Vicar of Detling, Kent, and for many years Curate of Lambeth Parish Church. With an Introduction by the Archbishop of Canterbury. Second Edition, containing an additional Chapter on Medieval Life in the Old Palaces. 8vo, with Illustrations, 21s.

CHARTERIS. Canonicity; or, Early Testimonies to the Existence and Use of the Books of the New Testament. Based on Kirchhoffer's 'Quellensammlung.' Edited by A. H. CHARTERIS, D.D., Professor of Biblical Criticism in the University of Edinburgh. 8vo, 18s.

CHIROL. 'Twixt Greek and Turk. By M. VALENTINE CHIROL. Post 8vo. With Frontispiece and Map, 10s. 6d.

CHRISTISON. Life of Sir Robert Christison, Bart., M.D., D.C.L. Oxon., Professor of Medical Jurisprudence in the University of Edinburgh. Edited by his SONS. In two vols. 8vo. Vol. I.—Autobiography. 16s. Vol. II.—Memoirs. *Shortly.*

CHURCH SERVICE SOCIETY. A Book on Common Order: Being Forms of Worship issued by the Church Service Society. Fourth Edition, 6s.

COCHRAN. A Handy Text-Book of Military Law. Compiled chiefly to assist Officers preparing for Examination; also for all Officers of the Regular and Auxiliary Forces. Specially arranged according to the Syllabus of Subjects of Examination for Promotion, Queen's Regulations, 1883. Comprising also a Synopsis of part of the Army Act. By MAJOR F. COCHRAN, Hampshire Regiment, Garrison Instructor, North British District. Crown 8vo, 7s. 6d.

COLQUHOUN. The Moor and the Loch. Containing Minute Instructions in all Highland Sports, with Wanderings over Crag and Corrie, Flood and Fell. By JOHN COLQUHOUN. Sixth Edition, greatly enlarged. With Illustrations. 2 vols. post 8vo, 26s.

COTTERILL. The Genesis of the Church. By the Right. Rev. HENRY COTTERILL, D.D., Bishop of Edinburgh. Demy 8vo, 16s.

COTTERILL. Suggested Reforms in Public Schools. By C. C. COTTERILL, M.A., Assistant Master at Fettes College, Edin. Crown 8vo, 3s. 6d.

COX. The Opening of the Line: A Strange Story of Dogs and their Doings. By PONSONBY COX. Profusely Illustrated by J. H. O. BROWN. 4to.

CRANSTOUN. The Elegies of Albius Tibullus. Translated into English Verse, with Life of the Poet, and Illustrative Notes. By JAMES CRANSTOUN, LL.D., Author of a Translation of 'Catullus.' Crown 8vo, 6s. 6d.

———— The Elegies of Sextus Propertius. Translated into English Verse, with Life of the Poet, and Illustrative Notes. Crown 8vo, 7s. 6d.

CRAWFORD. The Doctrine of Holy Scripture respecting the Atonement. By the late THOMAS J. CRAWFORD, D.D., Professor of Divinity in the University of Edinburgh. Third Edition. 8vo, 12s.

———— The Fatherhood of God, Considered in its General and Special Aspects, and particularly in relation to the Atonement, with a Review of Recent Speculations on the Subject. Third Edition, Revised and Enlarged. 8vo, 9s.

———— The Preaching of the Cross, and other Sermons. 8vo, 7s. 6d.

———— The Mysteries of Christianity. Crown 8vo, 7s. 6d.

DAVIES. A Book of Thoughts for every Day in the Year. Selected from the Writings of the Rev. J. LLEWELLYN DAVIES, M.A. By TWO CLERGYMEN. Fcap. 8vo, 3s. 6d.

DAVIES. Norfolk Broads and Rivers; or, The Waterways, Lagoons, and Decoys of East Anglia. By G. CHRISTOPHER DAVIES, Author of 'The Swan and her Crew.' Illustrated with Seven full-page Plates. New and Cheaper Edition. Crown 8vo, 6s.

DE AINSLIE. Life as I have Found It. By General DE AINSLIE. Post 8vo, 12s. 6d.

DESCARTES. The Method, Meditations, and Principles of Philosophy of Descartes. Translated from the Original French and Latin. With a New Introductory Essay, Historical and Critical, on the Cartesian Philosophy. By JOHN VEITCH, LL.D., Professor of Logic and Rhetoric in the University of Glasgow. A New Edition, being the Eighth. Price 6s. 6d.

DIDON. The Germans. By the Rev. Father DIDON, of the Order of Preaching Friars. Translated into English by RAPHAEL LEDOS DE BEAUFORT. Crown 8vo, 7s. 6d.

DOGS, OUR DOMESTICATED : Their Treatment in reference to Food, Diseases, Habits, Punishment, Accomplishments. By 'MAGENTA.' Crown 8vo, 2s. 6d.

DU CANE. The Odyssey of Homer, Books I.-XII. Translated into English Verse. By Sir CHARLES DU CANE, K.C.M.G. 8vo, 10s. 6d.

DUDGEON. History of the Edinburgh or Queen's Regiment Light Infantry Militia, now 3rd Battalion The Royal Scots; with an Account of the Origin and Progress of the Militia, and a Brief Sketch of the old Royal Scots. By Major R. C. DUDGEON, Adjutant 3rd Battalion The Royal Scots. Post 8vo, with Illustrations, 10s. 6d.

DUNSMORE. Manual of the Law of Scotland, as to the Relations between Agricultural Tenants and their Landlords, Servants, Merchants, and Bowers. By W. DUNSMORE, Advocate. 8vo, 7s. 6d.

DUPRE. Thoughts on Art, and Autobiographical Memoirs of Giovanni Duprè. Translated from the Italian by E. M. PERUZZI, with the permission of the Author. Crown 8vo, 10s. 6d.

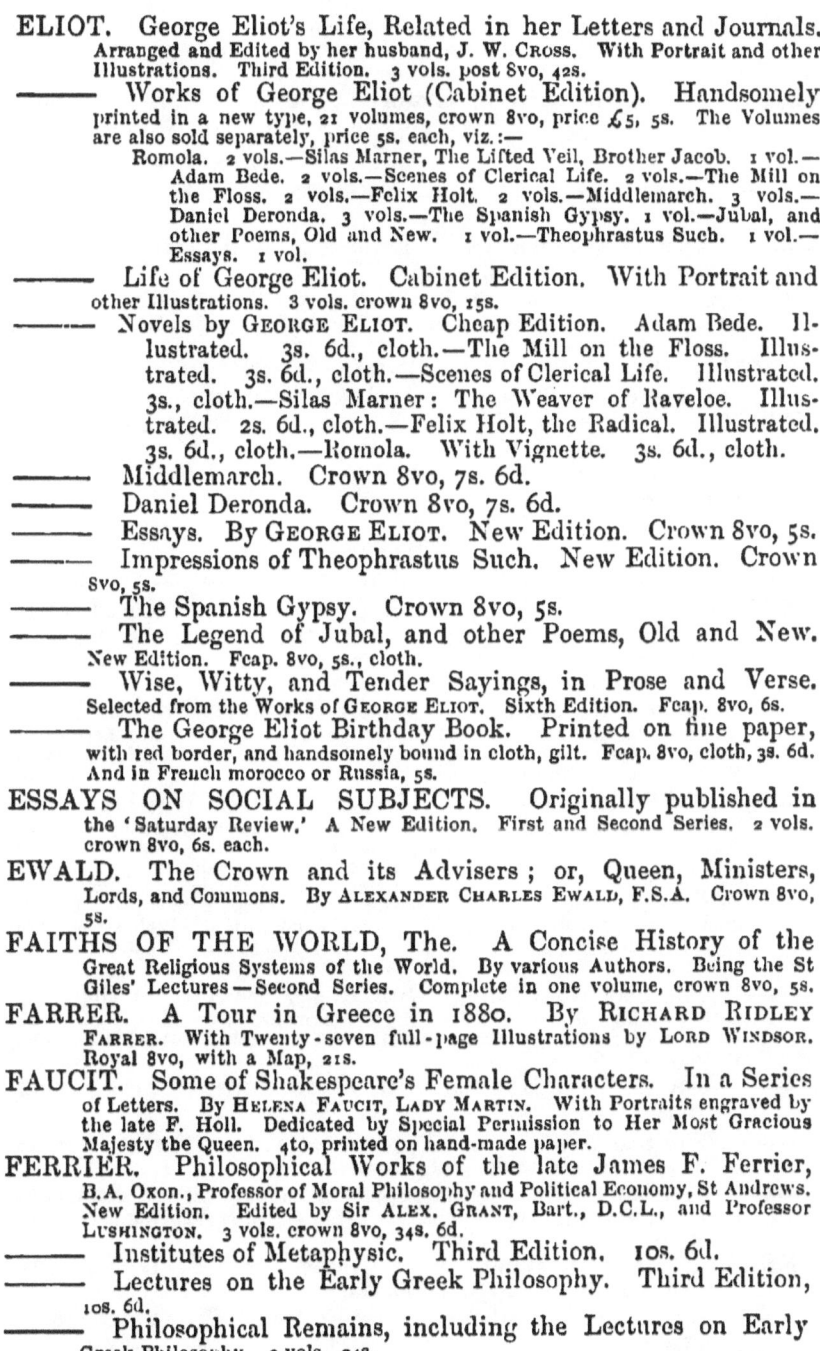

ELIOT. George Eliot's Life, Related in her Letters and Journals. Arranged and Edited by her husband, J. W. CROSS. With Portrait and other Illustrations. Third Edition. 3 vols. post 8vo, 42s.

———— Works of George Eliot (Cabinet Edition). Handsomely printed in a new type, 21 volumes, crown 8vo, price £5, 5s. The Volumes are also sold separately, price 5s. each, viz.:—
Romola. 2 vols.—Silas Marner, The Lifted Veil, Brother Jacob. 1 vol.—Adam Bede. 2 vols.—Scenes of Clerical Life. 2 vols.—The Mill on the Floss. 2 vols.—Felix Holt. 2 vols.—Middlemarch. 3 vols.—Daniel Deronda. 3 vols.—The Spanish Gypsy. 1 vol.—Jubal, and other Poems, Old and New. 1 vol.—Theophrastus Such. 1 vol.—Essays. 1 vol.

———— Life of George Eliot. Cabinet Edition. With Portrait and other Illustrations. 3 vols. crown 8vo, 15s.

———— Novels by GEORGE ELIOT. Cheap Edition. Adam Bede. Illustrated. 3s. 6d., cloth.—The Mill on the Floss. Illustrated. 3s. 6d., cloth.—Scenes of Clerical Life. Illustrated. 3s., cloth.—Silas Marner : The Weaver of Raveloe. Illustrated. 2s. 6d., cloth.—Felix Holt, the Radical. Illustrated. 3s. 6d., cloth.—Romola. With Vignette. 3s. 6d., cloth.

———— Middlemarch. Crown 8vo, 7s. 6d.

———— Daniel Deronda. Crown 8vo, 7s. 6d.

———— Essays. By GEORGE ELIOT. New Edition. Crown 8vo, 5s.

———— Impressions of Theophrastus Such. New Edition. Crown 8vo, 5s.

———— The Spanish Gypsy. Crown 8vo, 5s.

———— The Legend of Jubal, and other Poems, Old and New. New Edition. Fcap. 8vo, 5s., cloth.

———— Wise, Witty, and Tender Sayings, in Prose and Verse. Selected from the Works of GEORGE ELIOT. Sixth Edition. Fcap. 8vo, 6s.

———— The George Eliot Birthday Book. Printed on fine paper, with red border, and handsomely bound in cloth, gilt. Fcap. 8vo, cloth, 3s. 6d. And in French morocco or Russia, 5s.

ESSAYS ON SOCIAL SUBJECTS. Originally published in the 'Saturday Review.' A New Edition. First and Second Series. 2 vols. crown 8vo, 6s. each.

EWALD. The Crown and its Advisers ; or, Queen, Ministers, Lords, and Commons. By ALEXANDER CHARLES EWALD, F.S.A. Crown 8vo, 5s.

FAITHS OF THE WORLD, The. A Concise History of the Great Religious Systems of the World. By various Authors. Being the St Giles' Lectures — Second Series. Complete in one volume, crown 8vo, 5s.

FARRER. A Tour in Greece in 1880. By RICHARD RIDLEY FARRER. With Twenty-seven full-page Illustrations by LORD WINDSOR. Royal 8vo, with a Map, 21s.

FAUCIT. Some of Shakespeare's Female Characters. In a Series of Letters. By HELENA FAUCIT, LADY MARTIN. With Portraits engraved by the late F. Holl. Dedicated by Special Permission to Her Most Gracious Majesty the Queen. 4to, printed on hand-made paper.

FERRIER. Philosophical Works of the late James F. Ferrier, B.A. Oxon., Professor of Moral Philosophy and Political Economy, St Andrews. New Edition. Edited by Sir ALEX. GRANT, Bart., D.C.L., and Professor LUSHINGTON. 3 vols. crown 8vo, 34s. 6d.

———— Institutes of Metaphysic. Third Edition. 10s. 6d.

———— Lectures on the Early Greek Philosophy. Third Edition, 10s. 6d.

———— Philosophical Remains, including the Lectures on Early Greek Philosophy. 2 vols., 24s.

FLETCHER. Lectures on the Opening Clauses of the Litany delivered in St Paul's Church, Edinburgh. By JOHN B. FLETCHER, M.A. Crown 8vo, 4s.

FLINT. The Philosophy of History in Europe. Vol. I., containing the History of that Philosophy in France and Germany. By ROBERT FLINT, D.D., LL.D., Professor of Divinity, University of Edinburgh. 8vo. [*New Edition in preparation.*]

——— Theism. Being the Baird Lecture for 1876. Fourth Edition. Crown 8vo, 7s. 6d.

——— Anti-Theistic Theories. Being the Baird Lecture for 1877. Third Edition. Crown 8vo, 10s. 6d.

FORBES. The Campaign of Garibaldi in the Two Sicilies : A Personal Narrative. By CHARLES STUART FORBES, Commander, R.N. Post 8vo, with Portraits, 12s.

FOREIGN CLASSICS FOR ENGLISH READERS. Edited by Mrs OLIPHANT. Price 2s. 6d. *For List of Volumes issued, see p. 2.*

FRANZOS. The Jews of Barnow. Stories by KARL EMIL FRANZOS. Translated by M. W. MACDOWALL. Crown 8vo, 6s.

GALT. Annals of the Parish. By JOHN GALT. Fcap. 8vo, 2s.

——— The Provost. Fcap. 8vo, 2s.

——— Sir Andrew Wylie. Fcap. 8vo, 2s.

——— The Entail ; or, The Laird of Grippy. Fcap. 8vo, 2s.

GENERAL ASSEMBLY OF THE CHURCH OF SCOTLAND.

——— Family Prayers. Authorised by the General Assembly of the Church of Scotland. A New Edition, crown 8vo, in large type, 4s. 6d. Another Edition, crown 8vo, 2s.

——— Prayers for Social and Family Worship. For the Use of Soldiers, Sailors, Colonists, and Sojourners in India, and other Persons, at home and abroad, who are deprived of the ordinary services of a Christian Ministry. Cheap Edition, 1s. 6d.

——— The Scottish Hymnal. Hymns for Public Worship. Published for Use in Churches by Authority of the General Assembly. Various sizes—viz. : 1. Large type, for Pulpit use, cloth, 3s. 6d. 2. Longprimer type, cloth, red edges, 1s. 6d. ; French morocco, 2s. 6d. ; calf, 6s. 3. Bourgeois type, cloth, red edges, 1s. ; French morocco, 2s. 4. Minion type, limp cloth, 6d. ; French morocco, 1s. 6d. 5. School Edition, in paper cover, 2d. 6. Children's Hymnal, paper cover, 1d. No. 2, bound with the Psalms and Paraphrases, cloth, 3s. ; French morocco, 4s. 6d. ; calf, 7s. 6d. No. 3, bound with the Psalms and Paraphrases, cloth, 2s. ; French morocco, 3s.

——— The Scottish Hymnal, with Music. Selected by the Committees on Hymns and on Psalmody. The harmonies arranged by W. H. Monk. Cloth, 1s. 6d. ; French morocco, 3s. 6d. The same in the Tonic Sol-fa Notation, 1s. 6d. and 3s. 6d.

——— The Scottish Hymnal, with Fixed Tune for each Hymn. Longprimer type, 3s. 6d.

——— The Scottish Hymnal Appendix. 1. Longprimer type, 1s. 2. Nonpareil type, cloth limp, 4d.; paper cover, 2d.

——— Scottish Hymnal with Appendix Incorporated. Bourgeois type, limp cloth, 1s. Large type, cloth, red edges, 2s. 6d. Nonpareil type, paper covers, 3d. ; cloth, red edges, 6d.

GERARD. Reata : What's in a Name. By E. D. GERARD. New Edition. In one volume, crown 8vo, 6s.

——— Beggar my Neighbour. New Edition. Crown 8vo, 6s.

——— The Waters of Hercules. 3 vols. Post 8vo, 25s. 6d.

GOETHE'S FAUST. Translated into English Verse by Sir THEO-
DORE MARTIN, K.C.B. Second Edition, post 8vo, 6s. Cheap Edition, fcap.,
3s. 6d.

GOETHE. Poems and Ballads of Goethe. Translated by Professor
AYTOUN and Sir THEODORE MARTIN, K.C.B. Third Edition, fcap. 8vo, 6s.

GORDON CUMMING. At Home in Fiji. By C. F. GORDON
CUMMING, Author of 'From the Hebrides to the Himalayas.' Fourth Edition,
post 8vo. With Illustrations and Map. 7s. 6d.

——— A Lady's Cruise in a French Man-of-War. New and
Cheaper Edition. 8vo. With Illustrations and Map. 12s. 6d.

——— Fire-Fountains. The Kingdom of Hawaii : Its Volcanoes,
and the History of its Missions. With Map and numerous Illustrations. 2
vols. 8vo, 25s.

——— Granite Crags : The Yō-semité Region of California. Illustrated with 8 Engravings. One vol. 8vo, 16s.

——— Wanderings in China. 2 vols. 8vo, with Illustrations, 25s.

GRAHAM. The Life and Work of Syed Ahmed Khan, C.S.I.
By Lieut.-Colonel G. F. I. GRAHAM, B.S.C. 8vo, 14s.

GRANT. Bush-Life in Queensland. By A. C. GRANT. New
Edition. Crown 8vo, 6s.

HAMERTON. Wenderholme : A Story of Lancashire and York-
shire Life. By PHILIP GILBERT HAMERTON, Author of 'A Painter's Camp.' A
New Edition. Crown 8vo, 6s.

HAMILTON. Lectures on Metaphysics. By Sir WILLIAM HAMIL-
TON, Bart., Professor of Logic and Metaphysics in the University of Edinburgh.
Edited by the Rev. H. L. MANSEL, B.D., LL.D., Dean of St Paul's ; and JOHN
VEITCH, M.A., Professor of Logic and Rhetoric, Glasgow. Sixth Edition. 2
vols. 8vo, 24s.

——— Lectures on Logic. Edited by the SAME. Third Edition.
2 vols., 24s.

——— Discussions on Philosophy and Literature, Education and
University Reform. Third Edition, 8vo, 21s.

——— Memoir of Sir William Hamilton, Bart., Professor of Logic
and Metaphysics in the University of Edinburgh. By Professor VEITCH of the
University of Glasgow. 8vo, with Portrait, 18s.

——— Sir William Hamilton : The Man and his Philosophy.
Two Lectures Delivered before the Edinburgh Philosophical Institution,
January and February 1883. By the SAME. Crown 8vo, 2s.

HAMILTON. Annals of the Peninsular Campaigns. By Captain
THOMAS HAMILTON. Edited by F. Hardman. 8vo, 16s. Atlas of Maps to
illustrate the Campaigns, 12s.

HAMILTON. Mr Montenello. A Romance of the Civil Service.
By W. A. BAILLIE HAMILTON. In 3 vols. post 8vo, 25s. 6d.

HAMLEY. The Operations of War Explained and Illustrated. By
Lieut.-General Sir EDWARD BRUCE HAMLEY, K.C.M.G. Fourth Edition,
revised throughout. 4to, with numerous Illustrations, 30s.

——— Thomas Carlyle : An Essay. Second Edition. Crown
8vo. 2s. 6d.

——— The Story of the Campaign of Sebastopol. Written in the
Camp. With Illustrations drawn in Camp by the Author. 8vo, 21s.

——— On Outposts. Second Edition. 8vo, 2s.

——— Wellington's Career ; A Military and Political Summary.
Crown 8vo, 2s.

——— Lady Lee's Widowhood. Crown 8vo, 2s. 6d.

——— Our Poor Relations. A Philozoic Essay. With Illustrations, chiefly by Ernest Griset. Crown 8vo, cloth gilt, 3s. 6d.

HAMLEY. Guilty, or Not Guilty? A Tale. By Major-General W. G. HAMLEY, late of the Royal Engineers. New Edition. Crown 8vo, 3s. 6d.

—— Traseaden Hall. "When George the Third was King." New and Cheaper Edition. Crown 8vo, 6s.

HARBORD. Definitions and Diagrams in Astronomy and Navigation. By the Rev. J. B. HARBORD, M.A., Assistant Director of Education, Admiralty. 1s.

—— Short Sermons for Hospitals and Sick Seamen. Fcap. 8vo, cloth, 4s. 6d.

HARDMAN. Scenes and Adventures in Central America. Edited by FREDERICK HARDMAN. Crown 8vo. 6s.

HARRISON. Oure Tounis Colledge. Sketches of the History of the Old College of Edinburgh, with an Appendix of Historical Documents. By JOHN HARRISON. Crown 8vo, 5s.

HASELL. Bible Partings. By E. J. HASELL. Crown 8vo, 6s.

—— Short Family Prayers. By Miss HASELL. Cloth, 1s.

HAY. The Works of the Right Rev. Dr George Hay, Bishop of Edinburgh. Edited under the Supervision of the Right Rev. Bishop STRAIN. With Memoir and Portrait of the Author. 5 vols. crown 8vo, bound in extra cloth, £1, 1s. Or, sold separately,—viz.: The Sincere Christian Instructed in the Faith of Christ from the Written Word. 2 vols., 8s.—The Devout Christian Instructed in the Law of Christ from the Written Word. 2 vols., 8s.—The Pious Christian Instructed in the Nature and Practice of the Principal Exercises of Piety. 1 vol., 4s.

HEATLEY. The Horse-Owner's Safeguard. A Handy Medical Guide for every Man who owns a Horse. By G. S. HEATLEY, M.R.C., V.S. Crown 8vo, 5s.

—— The Stock-Owner's Guide. A Handy Medical Treatise for every Man who owns an Ox or a Cow. Crown 8vo, 4s. 6d.

HEMANS. The Poetical Works of Mrs Hemans. Copyright Editions.—One Volume, royal 8vo, 5s.—The Same, with Illustrations engraved on Steel, bound in cloth, gilt edges, 7s. 6d.—Six Volumes in Three, fcap., 12s. 6d. SELECT POEMS OF MRS HEMANS. Fcap., cloth, gilt edges, 3s.

HOBART PACHA. The Torpedo Scare; Experiences during the Turco-Russian War. By HOBART PACHA. Reprinted from 'Blackwood's Magazine,' with additional matter. Crown 8vo, 1s.

HOLE. A Book about Roses: How to Grow and Show Them. By the Rev. Canon HOLE. Ninth Edition, revised. Crown 8vo, 3s. 6d.

HOME PRAYERS. By Ministers of the Church of Scotland and Members of the Church Service Society. Second Edition. Fcap. 8vo, 3s.

HOMER. The Odyssey. Translated into English Verse in the Spenserian Stanza. By PHILIP STANHOPE WORSLEY. Third Edition, 2 vols. fcap., 12s.

—— The Iliad. Translated by P. S. WORSLEY and Professor CONINGTON. 2 vols. crown 8vo, 21s.

HOSACK. Mary Queen of Scots and Her Accusers. Containing a Variety of Documents never before published. By JOHN HOSACK, Barrister-at-Law. A New and Enlarged Edition, with a Photograph from the Bust on the Tomb in Westminster Abbey. 2 vols. 8vo, £1, 1s.

HYDE. The Royal Mail; its Curiosities and Romance. By JAMES WILSON HYDE, Superintendent in the General Post Office, Edinburgh. Second Edition, enlarged. Crown 8vo, with Illustrations, 6s.

INDEX GEOGRAPHICUS : Being a List, alphabetically arranged, of the Principal Places on the Globe, with the Countries and Subdivisions of the Countries in which they are situated, and their Latitudes and Longitudes. Applicable to all Modern Atlases and Maps. Imperial 8vo, pp. 676, 21s.

JEAN JAMBON. Our Trip to Blunderland ; or, Grand Excursion to Blundertown and Back. By JEAN JAMBON. With Sixty Illustrations designed by CHARLES DOYLE, engraved by DALZIEL. Fourth Thousand. Handsomely bound in cloth, gilt edges, 6s. 6d. Cheap Edition, cloth, 3s. 6d. In boards, 2s. 6d.

JOHNSON. The Scots Musical Museum. Consisting of upwards of Six Hundred Songs, with proper Basses for the Pianoforte. Originally published by JAMES JOHNSON ; and now accompanied with Copious Notes and Illustrations of the Lyric Poetry and Music of Scotland, by the late WILLIAM STENHOUSE ; with additional Notes and Illustrations, by DAVID LAING and C. K. SHARPE. 4 vols. 8vo, Roxburghe binding, £2, 12s. 6d.

JOHNSTON. The Chemistry of Common Life. By Professor J. F. W. JOHNSTON. New Edition, Revised, and brought down to date. By ARTHUR HERBERT CHURCH, M.A. Oxon. ; Author of 'Food : its Sources, Constituents, and Uses ;' 'The Laboratory Guide for Agricultural Students ;' 'Plain Words about Water,' &c. Illustrated with Maps and 102 Engravings on Wood. Complete in one volume, crown 8vo, pp. 618, 7s. 6d.

——— Elements of Agricultural Chemistry and Geology. Thirteenth Edition, Revised, and brought down to date. By Sir CHARLES A. CAMERON, M.D., F.R.C.S.I., &c. Fcap. 8vo, 6s. 6d.

——— Catechism of Agricultural Chemistry and Geology. An entirely New Edition, revised and enlarged, by Sir CHARLES A. CAMERON, M.D., F.R.C.S.I., &c. Eighty-first Thousand, with numerous Illustrations, 1s.

JOHNSTON. Patrick Hamilton : a Tragedy of the Reformation in Scotland, 1528. By T. P. JOHNSTON. Crown 8vo, with Two Etchings by the Author, 5s.

KENNEDY. Sport, Travel, and Adventures in Newfoundland and the West Indies. By Captain W. R. KENNEDY, R.N. With Illustrations by the Author. Post 8vo, 14s.

KING. The Metamorphoses of Ovid. Translated in English Blank Verse. By HENRY KING, M.A., Fellow of Wadham College, Oxford, and of the Inner Temple, Barrister-at-Law. Crown 8vo, 10s. 6d.

KINGLAKE. History of the Invasion of the Crimea. By A. W. KINGLAKE. Cabinet Edition. Seven Volumes, illustrated with maps and plans, crown 8vo, at 6s. each. The Volumes respectively contain :— I. THE ORIGIN OF THE WAR between the Czar and the Sultan. II. RUSSIA MET AND INVADED. III. THE BATTLE OF THE ALMA. IV. SEBASTOPOL AT BAY. V. THE BATTLE OF BALACLAVA. VI. THE BATTLE OF INKERMAN. VII. WINTER TROUBLES.

——— History of the Invasion of the Crimea. Vol. VI. Winter Troubles. Demy 8vo, with a Map, 16s.

——— History of the Invasion of the Crimea. Vol. VII. Demy 8vo. [In preparation.

——— Eothen. A New Edition, uniform with the Cabinet Edition of the 'History of the Crimean War,' price 6s.

KNOLLYS. The Elements of Field-Artillery. Designed for the Use of Infantry and Cavalry Officers. By HENRY KNOLLYS, Captain Royal Artillery ; Author of 'From Sedan to Saarbrück,' Editor of 'Incidents in the Sepoy War,' &c. With Engravings. Crown 8vo, 7s. 6d.

LAING. Select Remains of the Ancient Popular and Romance Poetry of Scotland. Originally Collected and Edited by DAVID LAING, LL.D. Re-edited, with Memorial-Introduction, by JOHN SMALL, M.A. With a Portrait of Dr Laing. 4to, 25s. The Edition has been limited to 350 copies.

LAVERGNE. The Rural Economy of England, Scotland, and Ireland. By LEONCE DE LAVERGNE. Translated from the French. With Notes by a Scottish Farmer. 8vo, 12s.

LEE. Lectures on the History of the Church of Scotland, from the Reformation to the Revolution Settlement. By the late Very Rev. JOHN LEE, D.D., LL.D., Principal of the University of Edinburgh. With Notes and Appendices from the Author's Papers. Edited by the Rev. WILLIAM LEE, D.D. 2 vols. 8vo, 21s.

LEE. Miss Brown: A Novel. By VERNON LEE. 3 vols. post 8vo, 25s. 6d.

LEE. Glimpses in the Twilight. Being various Notes, Records, and Examples of the Supernatural. By the Rev. GEORGE F. LEE, D.C.L. Crown 8vo. 8s. 6d.

LEE-HAMILTON. Poems and Transcripts. By EUGENE LEE-HAMILTON. Crown 8vo, 6s.

LEES. A Handbook of Sheriff Court Styles. By J. M. LEES, M.A., LL.B., Advocate, Sheriff-Substitute of Lanarkshire. 8vo, 16s.

——— A Handbook of the Sheriff and Justice of Peace Small Debt Courts. 8vo. 7s. 6d.

LETTERS FROM THE HIGHLANDS. Reprinted from 'The Times.' Fcap. 8vo, 4s. 6d.

LINDAU. The Philosopher's Pendulum and other Stories. By RUDOLPH LINDAU. Crown 8vo, 7s. 6d.

LITTLE. Madagascar: Its History and People. By the Rev. HENRY W. LITTLE, some years Missionary in East Madagascar. Post 8vo, 10s. 6d.

LOCKHART. Doubles and Quits. By LAURENCE W. M. LOCKHART. With Twelve Illustrations. Third Edition. Crown 8vo, 6s.

——— Fair to See: a Novel. Eighth Edition. Crown 8vo, 6s.

——— Mine is Thine: a Novel. Seventh Edition. Crown 8vo, 6s.

LORIMER. The Institutes of Law: A Treatise of the Principles of Jurisprudence as determined by Nature. By JAMES LORIMER, Regius Professor of Public Law and of the Law of Nature and Nations in the University of Edinburgh. New Edition, revised throughout, and much enlarged. 8vo, 18s.

——— The Institutes of the Law of Nations. A Treatise of the Jural Relation of Separate Political Communities. In 2 vols. 8vo. Volume I., price 16s. Volume II., price 20s.

M'COMBIE. Cattle and Cattle-Breeders. By WILLIAM M'COMBIE, Tillyfour. A New and Cheaper Edition, 2s. 6d., cloth.

MACRAE. A Handbook of Deer-Stalking. By ALEXANDER MACRAE, late Forester to Lord Henry Bentinck. With Introduction by HORATIO ROSS, Esq. Fcap. 8vo, with two Photographs from Life. 3s. 6d.

M'CRIE. Works of the Rev. Thomas M'Crie, D.D. Uniform Edition. Four vols. crown 8vo, 24s.

——— Life of John Knox. Containing Illustrations of the History of the Reformation in Scotland. Crown 8vo. 6s. Another Edition, 3s. 6d.

——— Life of Andrew Melville. Containing Illustrations of the Ecclesiastical and Literary History of Scotland in the Sixteenth and Seventeenth Centuries. Crown 8vo, 6s.

——— History of the Progress and Suppression of the Reformation in Italy in the Sixteenth Century. Crown 8vo, 4s.

——— History of the Progress and Suppression of the Reformation in Spain in the Sixteenth Century. Crown 8vo, 3s. 6d.

——— Lectures on the Book of Esther. Fcap. 8vo, 5s.

M'INTOSH. The Book of the Garden. By CHARLES M'INTOSH, formerly Curator of the Royal Gardens of his Majesty the King of the Belgians, and lately of those of his Grace the Duke of Buccleuch, K.G., at Dalkeith Palace. Two large vols. royal 8vo, embellished with 1350 Engravings. £4, 7s. 6d.
Vol. I. On the Formation of Gardens and Construction of Garden Edifices. 776 pages, and 1073 Engravings, £2, 10s.
Vol. II. Practical Gardening. 868 pages, and 279 Engravings, £1, 17s. 6d.

MACKAY. A Manual of Modern Geography; Mathematical, Physical, and Political. By the Rev. ALEXANDER MACKAY, LL.D., F.R.G.S. 11th Edition, revised to the present time. Crown 8vo, pp. 688. 7s. 6d.

—— Elements of Modern Geography. 51st Thousand, revised to the present time. Crown 8vo, pp. 300, 3s.

—— The Intermediate Geography. Intended as an Intermediate Book between the Author's 'Outlines of Geography' and 'Elements of Geography.' Tenth Edition, revised. Crown 8vo, pp. 224, 2s.

—— Outlines of Modern Geography. 170th Thousand, revised to the present time. 18mo, pp. 118, 1s.

—— First Steps in Geography. 82d Thousand. 18mo, pp. 56. Sewed, 4d.; cloth, 6d.

—— Elements of Physiography and Physical Geography. With Express Reference to the Instructions recently issued by the Science and Art Department. 25th Thousand, revised. Crown 8vo, 1s. 6d.

—— Facts and Dates; or, the Leading Events in Sacred and Profane History, and the Principal Facts in the various Physical Sciences. The Memory being aided throughout by a Simple and Natural Method. For Schools and Private Reference. New Edition. Crown 8vo, 3s. 6d.

MACKAY. An Old Scots Brigade. Being the History of Mackay's Regiment, now incorporated with the Royal Scots. With an Appendix containing many Original Documents connected with the History of the Regiment. By JOHN MACKAY (late) OF HERRIESDALE. Crown 8vo, 5s.

MACKAY. The Founders of the American Republic. A History of Washington, Adams, Jefferson, Franklin, and Madison. With a Supplementary Chapter on the Inherent Causes of the Ultimate Failure of American Democracy. By CHARLES MACKAY, LL.D. Post 8vo, 10s. 6d.

MACKELLAR. More Leaves from the Journal of a Life in the Highlands, from 1862 to 1882. Translated into Gaelic by Mrs MARY MACKELLAR. By command of Her Majesty the Queen. In one vol. crown 8vo, with Illustrations. [In the press.

MACKENZIE. Studies in Roman Law. With Comparative Views of the Laws of France, England, and Scotland. By LORD MACKENZIE, one of the Judges of the Court of Session in Scotland. Fifth Edition, Edited by JOHN KIRKPATRICK, Esq., M.A. Cantab.; Dr Jur. Heidelb.; LL.B., Edin.; Advocate. 8vo, 12s.

MADOC. Thereby. A Novel. By FAYR MADOC. Two vols. Post 8vo, 17s.

MAIN. Three Hundred English Sonnets. Chosen and Edited by DAVID M. MAIN. Fcap. 8vo, 6s.

MANNERS. Notes of an Irish Tour in 1846. By Lord JOHN MANNERS, M.P., G.C.B. New Edition. Crown 8vo, 2s. 6d.

MANNERS. Gems of German Poetry. Translated by Lady JOHN MANNERS. Small quarto, 3s. 6d.

—— Impressions of Bad-Homburg. Comprising a Short Account of the Women's Associations of Germany under the Red Cross. By Lady JOHN MANNERS. Crown 8vo, 1s. 6d.

—— Some Personal Recollections of the Later Years of the Earl of Beaconsfield, K.G. Sixth Edition, 6d.

MANNERS. Employment of Women in the Public Service. By Lady JOHN MANNERS. 6d.
——— Some of the Advantages of Easily Accessible Reading and Recreation Rooms, and Free Libraries. With Remarks on Starting and Maintaining Them. Crown 8vo, 1s.
——— A Sequel to Rich Men's Dwellings, and other Occasional Papers. Crown 8vo, 2s. 6d.

MARMORNE. The Story is told by ADOLPHUS SEGRAVE, the youngest of three Brothers. Third Edition. Crown 8vo, 6s.

MARSHALL. French Home Life. By FREDERIC MARSHALL. Second Edition. 5s.

MARSHMAN. History of India. From the Earliest Period to the Close of the India Company's Government; with an Epitome of Subsequent Events. By JOHN CLARK MARSHMAN, C.S.I. Abridged from the Author's larger work. Second Edition, revised. Crown 8vo, with Map, 6s. 6d.

MARTIN. Goethe's Faust. Translated by Sir THEODORE MARTIN, K.C.B. Second Edition, crown 8vo, 6s. Cheap Edition, 3s. 6d.
——— The Works of Horace. Translated into English Verse, with Life and Notes. In 2 vols. crown 8vo, printed on hand-made paper, 21s.
——— Poems and Ballads of Heinrich Heine. Done into English Verse. Second Edition. Printed on *papier vergé*, crown 8vo, 8s.
——— Catullus. With Life and Notes. Second Edition, post 8vo, 7s. 6d.
———. The Vita Nuova of Dante. With an Introduction and Notes. Second Edition, crown 8vo, 5s.
——— Aladdin : A Dramatic Poem. By ADAM OEHLENSCHLAE-GER. Fcap. 8vo, 5s.
——— Correggio : A Tragedy. By OEHLENSCHLAEGER. With Notes. Fcap. 8vo, 3s.
——— King Rene's Daughter : A Danish Lyrical Drama. By HENRIK HERTZ. Second Edition, fcap., 2s. 6d.

MARTIN. Some of Shakespeare's Female Characters. In a Series of Letters. By HELENA FAUCIT, LADY MARTIN. With Portraits engraved by the late F. Holl. Dedicated by Special Permission to Her Most Gracious Majesty the Queen. 4to, printed on hand-made paper.

MATHESON. Can the Old Faith Live with the New? or the Problem of Evolution and Revelation. By the Rev. GEORGE MATHESON, D.D., Inuellan. Crown 8vo, 7s. 6d.

MEIKLEJOHN. An Old Educational Reformer—Dr Bell. By J. M. D. MEIKLEJOHN, M.A., Professor of the Theory, History, and Practice of Education in the University of St Andrews. Crown 8vo, 3s. 6d.
——— The Golden Primer. With Coloured Illustrations by Walter Crane. Small 4to, boards, 5s.

MICHEL. A Critical Inquiry into the Scottish Language. With the view of Illustrating the Rise and Progress of Civilisation in Scotland. By FRANCISQUE-MICHEL, F.S.A. Lond. and Scot., Correspondant de l'Institut de France, &c. In One handsome Quarto Volume, printed on hand-made paper, and appropriately bound in Roxburghe style. Price 66s.

MICHIE. The Larch : Being a Practical Treatise on its Culture and General Management. By CHRISTOPHER Y. MICHIE, Forester, Cullen House. Crown 8vo, with Illustrations. New and Cheaper Edition, enlarged, 5s.

MILLIONAIRE, THE. By LOUIS J. JENNINGS, Author of 'Field Paths and Green Lanes,' 'Rambles among the Hills,' &c. Second Edition. 3 vols. crown 8vo, 25s. 6d.

MILNE. The Problem of the Churchless and Poor in our Large Towns. With special reference to the Home Mission Work of the Church of Scotland. By the Rev. ROBT. MILNE, M.A., Towie. Crown 8vo, 5s.

MINTO. A Manual of English Prose Literature, Biographical and Critical : designed mainly to show Characteristics of Style. By W. MINTO, M.A., Professor of Logic in the University of Aberdeen. Second Edition, revised. Crown 8vo, 7s. 6d.

—— Characteristics of English Poets, from Chaucer to Shirley. New Edition, revised. Crown 8vo, 7s. 6d.

MITCHELL. Biographies of Eminent Soldiers of the last Four Centuries. By Major-General JOHN MITCHELL, Author of 'Life of Wallenstein.' With a Memoir of the Author. 8vo, 9s.

MOIR. Life of Mansie Wauch, Tailor in Dalkeith. With 8 Illustrations on Steel, by the late GEORGE CRUIKSHANK. Crown 8vo, 3s. 6d. Another Edition, fcap. 8vo, 1s. 6d.

MOMERIE. Defects of Modern Christianity, and other Sermons. By the Rev. A. W. MOMERIE, M.A., D.Sc., Professor of Logic and Metaphysics in King's College, London. New Edition. Crown 8vo, 5s.

—— The Basis of Religion. Being an Examination of Natural Religion. Crown 8vo. 2s. 6d.

—— The Origin of Evil, and other Sermons. Fourth Edition, enlarged. Crown 8vo, 5s.

—— Personality. The Beginning and End of Metaphysics, and a Necessary Assumption in all Positive Philosophy. Second Edition. Crown 8vo, 3s.

—— Agnosticism, and other Sermons. Crown 8vo, 6s.

MONTAGUE. Campaigning in South Africa. Reminiscences of an Officer in 1879. By Captain W. E. MONTAGUE, 94th Regiment, Author of 'Claude Meadowleigh,' &c. 8vo, 10s. 6d.

MONTALEMBERT. Memoir of Count de Montalembert. A Chapter of Recent French History. By Mrs OLIPHANT, Author of the 'Life of Edward Irving,' &c. 2 vols. crown 8vo, £1, 4s.

MURDOCH. Manual of the Law of Insolvency and Bankruptcy : Comprehending a Summary of the Law of Insolvency, Notour Bankruptcy, Composition-contracts, Trust-deeds, Cessios, and Sequestrations; and the Winding-up of Joint-Stock Companies in Scotland; with Annotations on the various Insolvency and Bankruptcy Statutes; and with Forms of Procedure applicable to these Subjects. By JAMES MURDOCH, Member of the Faculty of Procurators in Glasgow. Fourth Edition, Revised and Enlarged, 8vo, £1.

MY TRIVIAL LIFE AND MISFORTUNE : A Gossip with no Plot in Particular By A PLAIN WOMAN. New Edition, crown 8vo, 6s.

NASEBY. Oaks and Birches. A Novel. By NASEBY. 3 vols. crown 8vo, 25s. 6d.

NEAVES. Songs and Verses, Social and Scientific. By an Old Contributor to 'Maga.' By the Hon. Lord NEAVES. Fifth Edition, fcap. 8vo, 4s.

—— The Greek Anthology. Being Vol. XX. of 'Ancient Classics for English Readers.' Crown 8vo, 2s. 6d.

NICHOLSON. A Manual of Zoology, for the Use of Students. With a General Introduction on the Principles of Zoology. By HENRY ALLEYNE NICHOLSON, M.D., D.Sc., F.L.S., F.G.S., Regius Professor of Natural History in the University of Aberdeen. Sixth Edition, revised and enlarged. Crown 8vo, pp. 816, with 394 Engravings on Wood, 14s.

—— Text-Book of Zoology, for the Use of Schools. Third Edition, enlarged. Crown 8vo, with 188 Engravings on Wood, 6s.

—— Introductory Text-Book of Zoology, for the Use of Junior Classes. Fifth Edition, revised and enlarged, with 156 Engravings, 3s.

—— Outlines of Natural History, for Beginners ; being Descriptions of a Progressive Series of Zoological Types. Third Edition, with Engravings, 1s. 6d.

—— A Manual of Palæontology, for the Use of Students. With a General Introduction on the Principles of Palæontology. Second Edition. Revised and greatly enlarged. 2 vols. 8vo, with 722 Engravings, £2, 2s.

NICHOLSON. The Ancient Life-History of the Earth. An Out-
line of the Principles and Leading Facts of Palæontological Science. By
HENRY ALLEYNE NICHOLSON, M.D., D.Sc., F.L.S., F.G.S , Regius Professor
of Natural History in the University of Aberdeen. Crown 8vo, with numerous
Engravings, 10s. 6d.

——— On the "Tabulate Corals" of the Palæozoic Period, with
Critical Descriptions of Illustrative Species. Illustrated with 15 Lithograph
Plates and numerous Engravings. Super-royal 8vo, 21s.

——— On the Structure and Affinities of the Genus Monticulipora
and its Sub-Genera, with Critical Descriptions of Illustrative Species. Illustrated with numerous Engravings on wood and lithographed Plates. Super-
royal 8vo, 18s.

——— Synopsis of the Classification of the Animal Kingdom.
8vo, with 106 Illustrations, 6s.

NICHOLSON. Communion with Heaven, and other Sermons.
By the late MAXWELL NICHOLSON, D.D., Minister of St Stephen's, Edinburgh.
Crown 8vo, 5s. 6d.

——— Rest in Jesus. Sixth Edition. Fcap. 8vo, 4s. 6d.

OLIPHANT. The Land of Gilead, With Excursions in the
Lebanon. By LAURENCE OLIPHANT, Author of 'Lord Elgin's Mission to
China and Japan,' &c. With Illustrations and Maps. Demy 8vo, 21s.

——— The Land of Khemi. Post 8vo, with Illustrations, 10s. 6d.

——— Sympneumata : or, Evolutionary Functions now Active in
Man. Post 8vo, 10s. 6d.

——— Altiora Peto. Seventh Edition, Illustrated. Crown 8vo, 6s.

——— Traits and Travesties ; Social and Political. Post 8vo, 10s. 6d.

——— Piccadilly: A Fragment of Contemporary Biography. With
Eight Illustrations by Richard Doyle. Fifth Edition, 4s. 6d. Cheap Edition,
in paper cover, 2s. 6d.

OLIPHANT. The Story of Valentine ; and his Brother. By Mrs
OLIPHANT. 5s., cloth.

——— Katie Stewart. 2s. 6d.

OSBORN. Narratives of Voyage and Adventure. By Admiral
SHERARD OSBORN, C.B. 3 vols. crown 8vo, 12s.

OSSIAN. The Poems of Ossian in the Original Gaelic. With a
Literal Translation into English, and a Dissertation on the Authenticity of the
Poems. By the Rev. ARCHIBALD CLERK. 2 vols. imperial 8vo, £1, 11s. 6d.

OSWALD. By Fell and Fjord ; or, Scenes and Studies in Iceland.
By E. J. OSWALD. Post 8vo, with Illustrations. 7s. 6d.

PAGE. Introductory Text-Book of Geology. By DAVID PAGE,
LL.D., Professor of Geology in the Durham University of Physical Science,
Newcastle. With Engravings on Wood and Glossarial Index. Eleventh
Edition, 2s. 6d.

——— Advanced Text-Book of Geology, Descriptive and Indus-
trial. With Engravings, and Glossary of Scientific Terms. Sixth Edition, revised and enlarged, 7s. 6d.

——— Geology for General Readers. A Series of Popular Sketches
in Geology and Palæontology. Third Edition, enlarged, 6s.

——— Introductory Text-Book of Physical Geography. With
Sketch-Maps and Illustrations. Edited by CHARLES LAPWORTH, F.G.S., &c.,
Professor of Geology and Mineralogy in the Mason Science College, Birming-
ham. 11th Edition. 2s. 6d.

——— Advanced Text-Book of Physical Geography. Third
Edition, Revised and Enlarged by Professor LAPWORTH. With Engravings.
5s.

PATON. Spindrift. By Sir J. NOEL PATON. Fcap., cloth, 5s.
—————— Poems by a Painter. Fcap., cloth, 5s.

PATTERSON. Essays in History and Art. By R. HOGARTH PATTERSON. 8vo, 12s.
—————— The New Golden Age, and Influence of the Precious Metals upon the World. 2 vols. 8vo, 31s. 6d.

PAUL. History of the Royal Company of Archers, the Queen's Body-Guard for Scotland. By JAMES BALFOUR PAUL, Advocate of the Scottish Bar. Crown 4to, with Portraits and other Illustrations. £2, 2s.

PAUL. Analysis and Critical Interpretation of the Hebrew Text of the Book of Genesis. Preceded by a Hebrew Grammar, and Dissertations on the Genuineness of the Pentateuch, and on the Structure of the Hebrew Language. By the Rev. WILLIAM PAUL, A.M. 8vo, 18s.

PETTIGREW. The Handy Book of Bees, and their Profitable Management. By A. PETTIGREW. Fourth Edition, Enlarged, with Engravings. Crown 8vo, 3s. 6d.

PHILOSOPHICAL CLASSICS FOR ENGLISH READERS. Companion Series to Ancient and Foreign Classics for English Readers. Edited by WILLIAM KNIGHT, LL.D., Professor of Moral Philosophy, University of St Andrews. In crown 8vo volumes, with portraits, price 3s. 6d.

1. DESCARTES. By Professor Mahaffy, Dublin.
2. BUTLER. By the Rev. W. Lucas Collins, M.A.
3. BERKELEY. By Professor A. Campbell Fraser, Edinburgh.
4. FICHTE. By Professor Adamson, Manchester.
5. KANT. By Professor Wallace, Oxford.
6. HAMILTON. By Professor Veitch, Glasgow.
7. HEGEL. By Professor Edward Caird, Glasgow.
8. LEIBNIZ. By J. Theodore Merz.
9. VICO. By Professor Flint, Edinburgh.
10. HOBBES. By Professor Croom Robertson, London.

POLLOK. The Course of Time : A Poem. By ROBERT POLLOK, A.M. Small fcap. 8vo, cloth gilt, 2s. 8d. The Cottage Edition, 32mo, sewed, 8d. The Same, cloth, gilt edges, 1s. 6d. Another Edition, with Illustrations by Birket Foster and others, fcap., gilt cloth, 3s. 6d., or with edges gilt, 4s.

PORT ROYAL LOGIC. Translated from the French : with Introduction, Notes, and Appendix. By THOMAS SPENCER BAYNES, LL.D., Professor in the University of St Andrews. Eighth Edition, 12mo, 4s.

POTTS AND DARNELL. Aditus Faciliores : An easy Latin Construing Book, with Complete Vocabulary. By A. W. POTTS, M.A., LL.D., Head-Master of the Fettes College, Edinburgh, and sometime Fellow of St John's College, Cambridge; and the Rev. C. DARNELL, M.A., Head-Master of Cargilfield Preparatory School, Edinburgh, and late Scholar of Pembroke and Downing Colleges, Cambridge. Eighth Edition, fcap. 8vo, 3s. 6d.

—————— Aditus Faciliores Graeci. An easy Greek Construing Book, with Complete Vocabulary. Third Edition, fcap. 8vo, 3s.

PRINGLE. The Live-Stock of the Farm. By ROBERT O. PRINGLE. Third Edition, crown 8vo. [In the press.

PRINGLE. Towards the Mountains of the Moon. A Journey in f East Africa. By Mrs Pringle of Whytbank, Yair. With a Map, 8vo, 12s. 6d.

PUBLIC GENERAL STATUTES AFFECTING SCOTLAND, from 1707 to 1847, with Chronological Table and Index. 3 vols. large 8vo, £3, 3s.

PUBLIC GENERAL STATUTES AFFECTING SCOTLAND, COLLECTION OF. Published Annually with General Index.

RAMSAY. Rough Recollections of Military Service and Society. By Lieut.-Col. BALCARRES D. WARDLAW RAMSAY. Two vols. post 8vo, 21s.

RAMSAY. Scotland and Scotsmen in the Eighteenth Century. From the MSS. of JOHN RAMSAY, Esq. of Ochtertyre. In two vols. 8vo. [In the press.

RANKINE.   A Treatise on the Rights and Burdens incident to the Ownership of Lands and other Heritages in Scotland. By JOHN RANKINE, M.A., Advocate. Second Edition, Revised and Enlarged. 8vo, 45s.

RECORDS OF THE TERCENTENARY FESTIVAL OF THE UNIVERSITY OF EDINBURGH. Celebrated in April 1884. Published under the Sanction of the Senatus Academicus. Large 4to, £2, 12s. 6d. *Only 150 copies printed for sale to the public.*

RIMMER.   The Early Homes of Prince Albert. By ALFRED RIMMER, Author of 'Our Old Country Towns,' &c. Beautifully Illustrated with Tinted Plates and numerous Engravings on Wood. 8vo, 21s.

ROBERTSON. Orellana, and other Poems. By J. LOGIE ROBERTSON, M.A. Fcap. 8vo. Printed on hand-made paper. 6s.

———   The White Angel of the Polly Ann, and other Stories. A Book of Fables and Fancies. Fcap. 8vo, 3s. 6d.

———   Our Holiday Among the Hills. By JAMES and JANET LOGIE ROBERTSON. Fcap. 8vo, 3s. 6d.

ROSCOE.   Rambles with a Fishing-rod. By E. S. ROSCOE. Crown 8vo, 4s. 6d.

ROSS.   Old Scottish Regimental Colours. By ANDREW ROSS, S.S.C., Hon. Secretary Old Scottish Regimental Colours Committee. Dedicated by Special Permission to Her Majesty the Queen. Folio, handsomely bound in cloth, £2, 12s. 6d.

RUSSELL.   The Haigs of Bemersyde. A Family History. By JOHN RUSSELL. Large 8vo, with Illustrations. 21s.

RUSSELL.   Reminiscences of Yarrow. By JAMES RUSSELL, D.D., late Minister of Yarrow. With a Preface by Professor CAMPBELL FRASER. In one vol. post 8vo.   [*In the press.*

RUSTOW.   The War for the Rhine Frontier, 1870 : Its Political and Military History. By Col. W. RUSTOW. Translated from the German, by JOHN LAYLAND NEEDHAM, Lieutenant R.M. Artillery. 3 vols. 8vo, with Maps and Plans, £1. 11s. 6d.

SCHETKY.   Ninety Years of Work and Play. Sketches from the Public and Private Career of JOHN CHRISTIAN SCHETKY, late Marine Painter in Ordinary to the Queen. By his DAUGHTER. Crown 8vo, 7s. 6d.

SCOTCH LOCH FISHING. By "Black Palmer." Crown 8vo, interleaved with blank pages, 4s.

SELLER AND STEPHENS.   Physiology at the Farm ; in Aid of Rearing and Feeding the Live Stock. By WILLIAM SELLER, M.D., F.R.S.E., Fellow of the Royal College of Physicians, Edinburgh, formerly Lecturer on Materia Medica and Dietetics ; and HENRY STEPHENS, F.R.S.E., Author of ' The Book of the Farm,' &c. Post 8vo, with Engravings, 16s.

SETON.   Memoir of Alexander Seton, Earl of Dunfermline, Seventh President of the Court of Session, and Lord Chancellor of Scotland. By GEORGE SETON, M.A. Oxon.; Author of the ' Law and Practice of Heraldry in Scotland,' &c. Crown 4to, 21s.

SETH.   Scottish Philosophy. A Comparison of the Scottish and German Answers to Hume. Balfour Philosophical Lectures, University of Edinburgh. By ANDREW SETH, M.A , Professor of Logic and Philosophy in the University College of South Wales and Monmouthshire. Crown 8vo, 5s.

SHADWELL.   The Life of Colin Campbell, Lord Clyde. Illustrated by Extracts from his Diary and Correspondence. By Lieutenant-General SHADWELL, C.B. 2 vols. 8vo. With Portrait, Maps, and Plans. 36s.

SHAND.   Letters from the West of Ireland. Reprinted from the ' Times.' By ALEXANDER INNES SHAND, Author of ' Letters from the West Highlands.' Crown 8vo, 5s.

SHARPE.   The Correspondence of Charles Kirkpatrick Sharpe. With a Memoir. In two vols. 8vo. Illustrated with Etchings and other Engravings.   [*In the press.*

SIM. Margaret Sim's Cookery. With an Introduction by L. B. WALFORD, Author of 'Mr Smith: A Part of His Life,' &c. Crown 8vo, 5s.

SIMPSON. Dogs of other Days: Nelson and Puck. By EVE BLANTYRE SIMPSON. Fcap. 8vo, with Illustrations, 2s. 6d.

SMITH. Italian Irrigation: A Report on the Agricultural Canals of Piedmont and Lombardy, addressed to the Hon. the Directors of the East India Company; with an Appendix, containing a Sketch of the Irrigation System of Northern and Central India. By Lieut.-Col. R. BAIRD SMITH, F.G.S., Captain, Bengal Engineers. Second Edition. 2 vols. 8vo, with Atlas, 30s.

SMITH. Thorndale; or, The Conflict of Opinions. By WILLIAM SMITH, Author of 'A Discourse on Ethics,' &c. A New Edition. Crown 8vo, 10s. 6d.

—— Gravenhurst; or, Thoughts on Good and Evil. Second Edition, with Memoir of the Author. Crown 8vo, 8s.

—— A Discourse on Ethics of the School of Paley. 8vo, 4s.

—— Dramas. 1. Sir William Crichton. 2. Athelwold. 3. Guidone. 24mo, boards, 3s.

SMITH. Greek Testament Lessons for Colleges, Schools, and Private Students, consisting chiefly of the Sermon on the Mount and the Parables of our Lord. With Notes and Essays. By the Rev. J. HUNTER SMITH, M.A., King Edward's School, Birmingham. Crown 8vo, 6s.

SMITH. Writings by the Way. By JOHN CAMPBELL SMITH, M.A., Sheriff-Substitute. Crown 8vo, 9s.

SMITH. The Secretary for Scotland. Being a Statement of the Powers and Duties of the new Scottish Office. With a Short Historical Introduction and numerous references to important Administrative Documents. By W. C. SMITH, LL.B., Advocate. 8vo, 6s.

SOLTERA. A Lady's Ride Across Spanish Honduras. By MARIA SOLTERA. With Illustrations. Post 8vo, 12s. 6d.

SORLEY. The Ethics of Naturalism. Being the Shaw Fellowship Lectures 1884. By W. R. Sorley, M.A., Fellow of Trinity College, Cambridge, and Examiner in Philosophy in the University of Edinburgh. Crown 8vo, 6s.

SOUTHEY. The Birthday, and other Poems. Second Edition, 5s.

—— Chapters on Churchyards. Fcap., 2s. 6d.

SPEKE. What led to the Discovery of the Nile Source. By JOHN HANNING SPEKE, Captain H.M. Indian Army. 8vo, with Maps, &c., 14s.

SPROTT. The Worship and Offices of the Church of Scotland; or, the Celebration of Public Worship, the Administration of the Sacraments, and other Divine Offices, according to the Order of the Church of Scotland. By GEORGE W. SPROTT, D.D., Minister of North Berwick. Crown 8vo, 6s.

STARFORTH. Villa Residences and Farm Architecture: A Series of Designs. By JOHN STARFORTH, Architect. 102 Engravings. Second Edition, medium 4to, £2, 17s. 6d.

STATISTICAL ACCOUNT OF SCOTLAND. Complete, with Index, 15 vols. 8vo, £16, 16s. Each County sold separately, with Title, Index, and Map, neatly bound in cloth, forming a very valuable Manual to the Landowner, the Tenant, the Manufacturer, the Naturalist, the Tourist, &c.

STEPHENS. The Book of the Farm; detailing the Labours of the Farmer, Farm-Steward, Ploughman, Shepherd, Hedger, Farm-Labourer, Field-Worker, and Cattleman. By HENRY STEPHENS, F.R.S.E. Illustrated with Portraits of Animals painted from the life; and with 557 Engravings on Wood, representing the principal Field Operations, Implements, and Animals treated of in the Work. A New and Revised Edition, the third, in great part Re-written. 2 vols. large 8vo, £2, 10s.

—— The Book of Farm Buildings; their Arrangement and Construction. By HENRY STEPHENS, F.R.S.E., Author of 'The Book of the Farm;' and ROBERT SCOTT BURN. Illustrated with 1045 Plates and Engravings. Large 8vo, uniform with 'The Book of the Farm,' &c. £1, 11s. 6d.

STEPHENS. The Book of Farm Implements and Machines. By J. SLIGHT and R. SCOTT BURN, Engineers. Edited by HENRY STEPHENS. Large 8vo, uniform with 'The Book of the Farm,' £2, 2s.

—— Catechism of Practical Agriculture. With Engravings. 1s.

STEWART. Advice to Purchasers of Horses. By JOHN STEWART, V.S., Author of 'Stable Economy.' 2s. 6d.

—— Stable Economy. A Treatise on the Management of Horses in relation to Stabling, Grooming, Feeding, Watering, and Working. Seventh Edition, fcap. 8vo, 6s. 6d.

STONE. Hugh Moore : a Novel. By EVELYN STONE. 2 vols. crown 8vo, 17s.

STORMONTH. Etymological and Pronouncing Dictionary of the English Language. Including a very Copious Selection of Scientific Terms. For Use in Schools and Colleges, and as a Book of General Reference. By the Rev. JAMES STORMONTH. The Pronunciation carefully Revised by the Rev. P. H. PHELP, M.A. Cantab. Eighth Edition, Revised throughout. Crown 8vo, pp. 800. 7s. 6d.

—— Dictionary of the English Language, Pronouncing, Etymological, and Explanatory. Revised by the Rev. P. H. PHELP. Library Edition. Imperial 8vo, handsomely bound in half morocco, 31s. 6d.

—— The School Etymological Dictionary and Word-Book. Combining the advantages of an ordinary pronouncing School Dictionary and an Etymological Spelling-book. Fcap. 8vo, pp. 254. 2s.

STORY. Nero ; A Historical Play. By W. W. STORY, Author of 'Roba di Roma.' Fcap. 8vo, 6s.

—— Vallombrosa. Post 8vo, 5s.

—— He and She ; or, A Poet's Portfolio. Fcap. 8vo, in parchment, 3s. 6d.

—— Poems. 2 vols., fcap., 7s. 6d.

—— Fiammetta. A Summer Idyl. Crown 8vo, 7s. 6d.

STURGIS. John-a-Dreams. A Tale. By JULIAN STURGIS. New Edition, crown 8vo, 3s. 6d.

—— Little Comedies, Old and New. Crown 8vo, 7s. 6d.

SUTHERLAND. Handbook of Hardy Herbaceous and Alpine Flowers, for general Garden Decoration. Containing Descriptions, in Plain Language, of upwards of 1000 Species of Ornamental Hardy Perennial and Alpine Plants, adapted to all classes of Flower-Gardens, Rockwork, and Waters ; along with Concise and Plain Instructions for their Propagation and Culture. By WILLIAM SUTHERLAND, Gardener to the Earl of Minto ; formerly Manager of the Herbaceous Department at Kew. Crown 8vo, 7s. 6d.

TAYLOR. The Story of My Life. By the late Colonel MEADOWS TAYLOR, Author of 'The Confessions of a Thug,' &c. &c. Edited by his Daughter. New and cheaper Edition, being the Fourth. Crown 8vo, 6s.

TEMPLE. Lancelot Ward, M.P. A Love-Story. By GEORGE TEMPLE. Crown 8vo. 7s. 6d.

THOLUCK. Hours of Christian Devotion. Translated from the German of A. Tholuck, D.D., Professor of Theology in the University of Halle. By the Rev. ROBERT MENZIES, D.D. With a Preface written for this Translation by the Author. Second Edition, crown 8vo, 7s. 6d.

THOMSON. Handy Book of the Flower-Garden : being Practical Directions for the Propagation, Culture, and Arrangement of Plants in Flower-Gardens all the year round. Embracing all classes of Gardens, from the largest to the smallest. With Engraved and Coloured Plans, illustrative of the various systems of Grouping in Beds and Borders. By DAVID THOMSON, Gardener to his Grace the Duke of Buccleuch, K.G., at Drumlanrig. Third Edition, crown 8vo, 7s. 6d.

THOMSON. The Handy Book of Fruit-Culture under Glass : being a series of Elaborate Practical Treatises on the Cultivation and Forcing of Pines, Vines, Peaches, Figs, Melons, Strawberries, and Cucumbers. With Engravings of Hothouses, &c., most suitable for the Cultivation and Forcing of these Fruits. By DAVID THOMSON, Gardener to his Grace the Duke of Buccleuch, K.G., at Drumlanrig. Second Edition. Crown 8vo, with Engravings, 7s. 6d.

THOMSON. A Practical Treatise on the Cultivation of the Grape-Vine. By WILLIAM THOMSON, Tweed Vineyards. Tenth Edition, 8vo, 5s.

TOM CRINGLE'S LOG. A New Edition, with Illustrations. Crown 8vo, cloth gilt, 5s. Cheap Edition, 2s.

TRANSACTIONS OF THE HIGHLAND AND AGRICUL-TURAL SOCIETY OF SCOTLAND. Published annually, price 5s.

TROLLOPE. An Autobiography by Anthony Trollope. Two Volumes, post 8vo, with Portrait. Second Edition. Price 21s.

—— The Fixed Period. 2 vols. fcap. 8vo, 12s.

—— An Old Man's Love. 2 vols. crown 8vo, 12s.

TULLOCH. Rational Theology and Christian Philosophy in Eng-land in the Seventeenth Century. By JOHN TULLOCH, D.D., Principal of St Mary's College in the University of St Andrews; and one of her Majesty's Chaplains in Ordinary in Scotland. Second Edition. 2 vols. 8vo, 28s.

—— Modern Theories in Philosophy and Religion. 8vo, 15s.

—— The Christian Doctrine of Sin ; being the Croall Lecture for 1876. Crown 8vo, 6s.

—— Theism. The Witness of Reason and Nature to an All-Wise and Beneficent Creator. 8vo, 10s. 6d.

—— Luther, and other Leaders of the Reformation. Third Edition, enlarged. Crown 8vo, 7s. 6d.

TWO STORIES OF THE SEEN AND THE UNSEEN. 'THE OPEN DOOR,' 'OLD LADY MARY.' Crown 8vo, cloth, 2s. 6d.

VEITCH. Institutes of Logic. By JOHN VEITCH, LL.D., Pro-fessor of Logic and Rhetoric in the University of Glasgow. Post 8vo, 12s. 6d.

VIRGIL. The Æneid of Virgil. Translated in English Blank Verse by G. K. RICKARDS, M.A., and Lord RAVENSWORTH. 2 vols. fcap. 8vo, 10s.

WALFORD. The Novels of L. B. WALFORD. New and Uniform Edition. Crown 8vo, each 5s.

MR SMITH: A PART OF HIS LIFE.	TROUBLESOME DAUGHTERS.
COUSINS.	DICK NETHERBY.
PAULINE.	THE BABY'S GRANDMOTHER.

—— Nan, and other Stories. 2 vols. crown 8vo, 12s.

WARDEN. Poems. By FRANCIS HEYWOOD WARDEN. With a Notice by Dr Vanroth. Crown 8vo, 5s.

WARREN'S (SAMUEL) WORKS. People's Edition, 4 vols. crown 8vo, cloth, 15s. 6d. Or separately :—

Diary of a Late Physician. Cloth, 2s. 6d. ; boards, 2s. Illus-trated, crown 8vo, 7s 6d.

Ten Thousand A-Year. Cloth, 3s. 6d. ; boards, 2s. 6d.

Now and Then. The Lily and the Bee. Intellectual and Moral Development of the Present Age. 4s. 6d.

Essays : Critical, Imaginative, and Juridical. 5s.

WARREN. The Five Books of the Psalms. With Marginal Notes. By Rev. SAMUEL L. WARREN, Rector of Esher, Surrey ; late Fellow, Dean, and Divinity Lecturer, Wadham College, Oxford. Crown 8vo, 5s.

WATSON. Christ's Authority ; and other Sermons. By the late ARCHIBALD WATSON, D.D., Minister of the Parish of Dundee, and one of Her Majesty's Chaplains for Scotland. With Introduction by the Very Rev. PRINCIPAL CAIRD, Glasgow. Crown 8vo, 7s. 6d.

WEBSTER. The Angler and the Loop-Rod. By DAVID WEBSTER. Crown 8vo, with Illustrations, 7s. 6d.

WELLINGTON. Wellington Prize Essays on "the System of Field Manœuvres best adapted for enabling our Troops to meet a Continental Army." Edited by Lieut.-General Sir EDWARD BRUCE HAMLEY, K.C.M.G. 8vo, 12s. 6d.

WESTMINSTER ASSEMBLY. Minutes of the Westminster Assembly, while engaged in preparing their Directory for Church Government, Confession of Faith, and Catechisms (November 1644 to March 1649). Edited by the Rev. Professor ALEX. T. MITCHELL, of St Andrews, and the Rev. JOHN STRUTHERS, LL.D. With a Historical and Critical Introduction by Professor Mitchell. 8vo, 15s.

WHITE. The Eighteen Christian Centuries. By the Rev. JAMES WHITE. Seventh Edition, post 8vo, with Index. 6s.

—— History of France, from the Earliest Times. Sixth Thousand, post 8vo, with Index, 6s.

WHITE. Archæological Sketches in Scotland—Kintyre and Knapdale. By Captain T. P. WHITE, R.E., of the Ordnance Survey. With numerous Illustrations. 2 vols. folio, £4, 4s. Vol. I., Kintyre, sold separately, £2, 2s.

WILLS AND GREENE. Drawing-room Dramas for Children. By W. G. WILLS and the Hon. Mrs GREENE. Crown 8vo, 6s.

WILSON. Works of Professor Wilson. Edited by his Son-in-Law Professor FERRIER. 12 vols. crown 8vo, £2, 8s.

—— Christopher in his Sporting-Jacket. 2 vols., 8s.

—— Isle of Palms, City of the Plague, and other Poems. 4s.

—— Lights and Shadows of Scottish Life, and other Tales. 4s.

—— Essays, Critical and Imaginative. 4 vols., 16s.

—— The Noctes Ambrosianæ. Complete, 4 vols., 14s.

—— The Comedy of the Noctes Ambrosianæ. By CHRISTOPHER NORTH. Edited by JOHN SKELTON, Advocate. With a Portrait of Professor Wilson and of the Ettrick Shepherd, engraved on Steel. Crown 8vo, 7s. 6d.

—— Homer and his Translators, and the Greek Drama. Crown 8vo, 4s.

WILSON. From Korti to Khartum: A Journal of the Desert March from Korti to Gubat and of the Ascent of the Nile in General Gordon's Steamers. By Colonel Sir CHARLES W. WILSON, K.C.B., K.C.M.G., R.E. Crown 8vo, 7s. 6d.

WINGATE. Annie Weir, and other Poems. By DAVID WINGATE. Fcap. 8vo, 5s.

—— Lily Neil. A Poem. Crown 8vo, 4s. 6d.

WORDSWORTH. The Historical Plays of Shakspeare. With Introductions and Notes. By CHARLES WORDSWORTH, D.C.L., Bishop of S. Andrews. 3 vols. post 8vo, each price 7s. 6d.

—— A Discourse on Scottish Church History. From the Reformation to the Present Time. With Prefatory Remarks on the St Giles' Lectures, and Appendix of Notes and References. Crown 8vo, cloth, 2s. 6d.

WORSLEY. Poems and Translations. By PHILIP STANHOPE WORSLEY, M.A. Edited by EDWARD WORSLEY. Second Edition, enlarged. Fcap. 8vo, 6s.

WYLDE. An Ill-Regulated Mind. A Novel. By KATHARINE WYLDE, Author of 'A Dreamer.' Crown 8vo, 7s. 6d.

YOUNG. Songs of Béranger done into English Verse. By WILLIAM YOUNG. New Edition, revised. Fcap. 8vo, 4s. 6d.

YULE. Fortification: for the Use of Officers in the Army, and Readers of Military History. By Col. YULE, Bengal Engineers. 8vo, with numerous Illustrations, 10s. 6d.